Okatibbee Creek

Lori Crane

Published by Lori Crane Entertainment

www.LoriCrane.com

This book is a work of historical fiction. Some names,
characters, places, and incidents are from historical accounts. Some
names, characters, places, and incidents are products of the author's
imagination.

ISBN-13: 978-0988354500
eBook ISBN: 978-0988354517

Table of Contents

In loving memory of
Mary Ann Rodgers
March 17, 1828 – July 18, 1898

For those who have come before. We are the living proof of their courage. We are their legacy. We are evidence of their resilience and their integrity, as well as their heartaches and sorrows. We are the children our grandmothers fought so hard for, for our safety, our lives, and our freedom, and who sacrificed everything with the depth of their love and their astounding resolve.

September 1834, Mississippi

"Help! Help! Somebody! James! Susannah!"

We all run as fast as we can down the creek toward the screaming, hopping over rocks and stumps and each other. When we arrive at the clearing, we see him next to the creek, dripping wet, on his hands and knees over the lifeless body of William. About twenty feet away lies Stephen, his clothes soaking wet, his head cocked to one side, and his left arm bent uncomfortably under his back. His lifeless eyes are staring into the darkening treetops.

Susannah starts screaming, but everyone ignores her. James runs directly to Stephen, picks him up by his shoulders, and starts shaking him, but it is painfully obvious that our Stephen is gone. His lips are blue. He isn't moving. He isn't breathing.

James yells at Susannah to stop screaming, and to run to the house and get Daddy. Susannah doesn't move, but her screaming quiets to a whimper.

James stands up and yells at her again. "Go, Susannah, go! Go get Daddy!"

I feel ice in my veins at the tone of James's voice. Susannah still doesn't move.

One of my brothers runs over to James's side and starts to pick up Stephen under his arms. "Help me pick him up, James. We don't have time for Susannah to go all the way there and back! Let's just get them back to the house," he urges.

They lift Stephen and carry his body toward the darkening woods, in the direction that leads back to the house. My other brothers follow their lead, pick William up under his arms and legs, and quickly move in the same direction.

Susannah stands frozen like a statue in the same spot, whimpering with her hands over her mouth. I run up behind her and nudge her toward the woods.

"Let's go, Sue. We have to run."

She doesn't move. She's white as a sheet. I push harder with my trembling hands. "Sue! Now! Let's go!"

An Ordinary Sunday

"Come on, Miss Mary, it's time to get up."

I lie still with my eyes closed, hoping she will go away.

A moment later, I feel her hand on my ankle, gently wiggling it as she coaxes me. "Come on, baby girl, rise and shine before your daddy comes in here to see why you're not up yet."

I open my eyes and look at her in the dim morning light.

"My daddy won't come in here." I grin at her and stick my tongue in the space where my tooth used to be.

She smiles at me as she lights the candle by the bed. She then picks up dirty stockings from the dirt floor as she continues, "Well, let's not wait and find out. We have to get you out of that bed and dressed before Old Sam comes to take us to Sunday service. I already have some biscuits and sowbelly on the table for your breakfast. Come on, baby girl, get up now."

As she speaks, she is moving toward the door with the dirty stockings in her hand and is almost knocked down by my sister Susannah, who flies through the old pine door and comes barreling into the room like a tornado.

Susannah leaps onto the feather bed.

Even though we share a bed, I didn't hear her get up this morning, and she is already fully dressed in her pale pink Sunday dress, with her dark hair tied in a braid and her shoes on. Susannah and I share a room with a couple of younger brothers. Looking around the room, I notice that I am the only one still in bed. I listen and hear them all in the kitchen talking with Momma, but our feather bed, with its blue and green patchwork quilt, is so comfortable and warm, I hate to crawl out of it.

"Get up, sleepyhead. Let's go!" Susannah yells. "It's a beautiful day outside, and as soon as church is over, James said he will take us down to the creek to go swimming and hunt for crawdads for supper." She bounces up and down on our squeaky bed like a rabbit.

"Okay, okay, I'm awake." I yawn as I stretch like a cat and sit up.

Susannah is my only sister. She is a tall and thin twelve-year-old with dark hair and pale blue eyes, just like most of my family. Momma calls her rambunctious. Bertie says right now Susannah is twice as old as me, and that will never, ever happen again. I am six.

Bertie is our house slave. Daddy got her just a few months ago, but she fits in so well with our family that it seems as if she has always been here. Bertie won't tell me how old she is, even though I've asked her a thousand times. I think she must be older than Momma, because she has a little gray in her hair, and gray hair is for old people. Momma doesn't have any gray in her hair.

Bertie is wafer-thin, with long, bony fingers

that feel funny when she gives me a bath or washes my hair. And they look funny when she points at something, like they are a little crooked or something. She has a singing voice like a bird's, and she can cook up a storm. I don't know how Momma did everything by herself before Bertie came. Bertie does everything and takes care of everyone. She is a sweet and funny woman, and I love her dearly, like she is my second mother.

After finishing my breakfast, Bertie helps me get into my blue Sunday dress. I only have one Sunday dress, and it is a hand-me-down from Susannah, but Momma says she is going to make me and Susannah some new dresses very soon. I told her I want a yellow dress.

When I finish dressing, Bertie washes my face and braids my hair. She is putting on my day cap when we hear Old Sam pull up to the front of the house in the wagon and yell "Whoa!" to the horses.

Suddenly, the house sounds like a stampede. We all charge out of the front door at the same time and climb up onto the wagon to go to church. Old Sam drives Daddy and Momma, Bertie, me and Susannah, and eight—yes, eight—brothers down the old path toward the church. My brother James, in his suspenders and vest, sits next to me. James is always hovering over me like he's my guardian angel or something. The oldest, Lewis, sits in the back with the younger boys—William, Stephen, and Timothy. William and Stephen sit next to each other, as close to the edge as they can, and whisper between themselves. Four-year-old Timothy, who loves to be with any family member who will pay him the slightest bit of attention, is sitting so close to Lewis, he's almost up in Lewis's lap. Little Hays Jr., who is two, sits on Daddy's lap with Daddy's strong arm around him. My older brothers, Allen and Jackson, sit in front with Old Sam, asking him over and over if they can hold the reins.

Old Sam is Daddy's farm slave. He helps Daddy with the plowing and planting, and is always chopping wood or getting water from the spring or mending a broken fence. He is a quiet man with a face full of lines that Momma says give him character. He doesn't have a beard like the other men I see. He can whistle better than anyone I've ever heard whistle, and sometimes when Bertie is in the house humming while she works, I can hear Old Sam out in the yard whistling along with her tune. I think Old Sam likes Bertie, but I don't think she likes him back.

The best thing about Old Sam is he is always patient with us children. He teaches us how to do things around the farm, and he gives us the feeling that nothing is more important to him than spending time with us doing that. He taught me how to fish and how to put a worm on a hook. I wonder sometimes if Old Sam has any children of his own, but I have never asked him. In the front of the old wooden wagon on this sunny Sunday morning, Old Sam lets the boys hold the reins all they want.

The ride to church is bumpy, long, dry, and dusty. Daddy says this old road, which isn't much of a road, used to be an old Indian trail. I'm glad we don't see Indians here now, because I'm a little afraid of Indians. Daddy tells me that the Indians who live around here are friendly, but Grandpa and Grandma Rodgers were picked on by mean Indians at their old house in Alabama. The Indians in Alabama were not nice, and they stole Grandpa's livestock and even burnt down Grandpa and Grandma's house. Those are the only Indian stories I have ever heard, so I guess that's why I am a little afraid of them. Daddy told me that is why we live here now, because there are no mean Indians here. I am totally lost in the thought of nice Indians and mean Indians when we finally pull up in front of the church.

Old Sam stops the wagon right in front of the church door by yelling a mighty "Whoa!" to the horses. The horses whinny and neigh as they stop, pulling against the reins. The boys immediately jump down from the wagon and run inside. At the same time, with one arm still holding little Hays Jr., Daddy jumps down and helps Momma from the wagon, while Old Sam helps Susannah, and James helps me. Then Old Sam walks around to the back of the wagon and puts out his hand for Bertie, but she pushes it aside and climbs down by herself. After Bertie lands solidly on the ground, she fans herself with one hand and wipes the dust from the skirt of her dark brown dress with the other hand.

"Whew, it's going to be a scorcher today," she says to no one in particular.

Old Sam shakes his head and sighs at her, as he climbs back up on the front of the wagon to move it and the horses around to the back of the church. With a click of his mouth and a snap of the reins, Old Sam and the wagon disappear around the corner.

Momma goes up the stone steps to the

wooden covered porch of the church, sighing out loud as she enters the refuge of the shade. She fans herself with a fan she made of dried ferns and herbs. I watch her as she reaches inside her high neckline and pulls it from her skin, stretching her neck the opposite way.

Daddy rolls his eyes at her and says, "Yes, ma'am, it is already too hot for this early in the day. Let's get this done and over with so we can get out of this hot-house."

Now it is Momma's turn to roll her eyes at him and his lack of respect for church.

Just like Daddy's usual reaction to her, he laughs at her eye-rolling, and then winks at me, and through his long beard, he grins. I don't know if his grin is for me or for his own pleasure that he irritated Momma once again. That is one of his favorite things to do — pick on Momma.

Daddy is all business all the time, except when it comes to Momma. He always teases her and I think she likes it. It's like they are in their own club and no one else is invited.

Daddy looks up at the roof of the covered porch and says, "Maybe we should think about building a new church, one with windows and a higher ceiling."

"Sure, Hays, that is a good idea, but you'll need to wait until after the harvest when it gets a little cooler," Momma says as she fans faster.

She pulls at her neckline once again, and keeps fanning herself as they enter the small log house.

Our church is made of sweet-gum logs, with a

dirt and sawdust floor. It is on Mr. Carpenter's land, but he says he doesn't know who built it or exactly how long it has been here. He says it was already here when he moved onto the land, which wasn't very long ago.

The Carpenter family moved here from Alabama. They have ten children just like our family, so when the Carpenters and the Rodgers all pile into church, it gets pretty full pretty fast. And that's before anyone else comes. There are the Sanderfords, the Calhouns, the Paces, the Blanks, and many more families who attend Fellowship Baptist Church.

The ceiling of our church is a pretty good height to let the heat rise, but there are no windows, only a front door and a back door. So, in the summertime, if the wind isn't blowing perfectly from front to back or back to front, it can get mighty hot in there. And if the wind is blowing just right, it blows out all the candles, leaving us sitting in the dark. Maybe Daddy is right—we do need windows.

Our church has two rooms. Some of the men made a podium for the preacher and some pews that fill up one of the rooms, though most of the time, the children just sit on the floor and the men stand in the back. The other room has some benches for the slaves. They are not allowed to sit with the rest of us in the main room.

Momma told me our church got started when Mrs. Carpenter and some of the neighbor ladies got together and decided they should form one. They say it will keep us "civilized." But something about the whole thing doesn't seem civilized to me.

The few friendly Indians who live on the

outskirts of our community are not welcome in the church. Why can't the Indians come and sing and hear Bible stories with us? But it really doesn't bother me so much that the Indians aren't welcome.

The slaves from the community are welcome, but they have to sit in the other room. Why can't Bertie sit next to me to sing songs and listen to the Bible? She sings really good, and I know she knows the Bible because she recites it all the time.

And there seems to be some sort of feud between a few members who think the church should minister to outsiders, and others who think the only reason for church is to read the Bible and leave everyone else alone. We learned one Sunday that the Bible says to love each other, so why are church members fighting amongst themselves? That doesn't seem very loving to me.

At the age of six, I guess I don't really understand what all these issues are about, but something about it all doesn't seem right to me. It certainly doesn't make any sense.

When it isn't Sunday, we use the gum-log building for school. Daddy and the neighbors thought it would be a good idea for us children to learn to read and write, so they got together and decided to start a school. One of the men from town, Mr. Brown, offered to teach if the parents would pay him a bit. The parents agreed and Mr. Brown started teaching.

He is a nice man. He is very, very tall and thin, and always wears a tall black hat to school, making him look taller than he already is. I love Mr. Brown and I love school, except when it is too hot.

We have school most of the time, but we take a couple weeks off in the spring for planting and again in the fall for harvesting. Since Susannah and I don't help the boys with planting or harvesting, we are usually dying of boredom while the boys work in the fields, and we can't wait for school to start again.

Sure, there is always plenty for us to do around the house to help Momma and Bertie. There are always little ones to watch, which is dull. There is butter to churn, which is the most boring job in the whole world and always given to the youngest. Since my little brothers, Hays Jr. and Timothy, are two and four and too young to churn, I get stuck with the churning most of the time.

There is the garden to tend, but sometimes there are more bugs and snakes out there than vegetables, and if I have to work in the garden, I'd rather churn butter.

There are chickens in the back of the yard to take care of. I don't mind cleaning out their roosts, but if they think I have food, they'll peck at my toes, which really hurts. I almost kicked one last week when she pecked me right on the ankle, but then I saw Old Sam watching me so I decided not to.

There is always sewing to be done, and sometimes Momma will let Susannah help her, but she says I am still too young to sew. She says to be patient and my time will come. I don't really like to be patient so much.

At our Sunday morning service, we sing a few songs and then listen to Reverend Jones give a sermon about Jesus and his disciples. During the church service, Momma goes into labor, but she doesn't tell anyone. By the time we make the long and bumpy trip back to the house, Momma is pretty uncomfortable. Riding in a wagon over an old bumpy Indian trail while in labor must seem to her like a longer and bumpier trip than usual.

When we finally arrive back at the house, Daddy and Old Sam help Momma into her room. I giggle as I watch Bertie scurry around, gathering cloth, water, and candles, humming the hymn we sang at church this morning.

Even though it is so hot outside, Old Sam carries in a bundle of firewood. I figure it will be used for light, not heat, in the fireplace if Momma doesn't give birth before nightfall. I can't think of any other reason to be lighting a fire inside the house today. Bertie won't even cook inside on a day like today. She would use the outdoor kitchen to make supper, and we would eat outside under the shade of the big maple trees.

I watch Old Sam carefully stack up the firewood next to the fireplace. Then Bertie asks him to go out and get a couple of buckets of water from the spring. Old Sam nods and heads out the back door. He gently closes it behind him, making sure it doesn't slam.

Bertie then turns her attention to us. "You girls run and change out of your Sunday clothes, and go down to the creek with your brothers. Your momma will be just fine. Bertie has birthed many babies, and I'm going to take good care of your momma. You all stay down at the creek as long as you want today, and give your momma some peace and quiet," Bertie orders. "I'll send Old Sam down there later with some butterbeans and cornbread for your supper."

With that, Bertie disappears behind the closed bedroom door with Momma. I stare at the door for a minute, wondering if Momma will have a girl today. I would love a little sister to play with.

After we all change our clothes, Susannah and I head to the creek with Lewis, James, Allen, and Jackson—our oldest brothers. The youngest boys, Timothy and Hays Jr. went home after church service with Reverend and Mrs. Jones for the day. The middle boys, Stephen and William, say they are going to mess around in the woods with a new slingshot they made, and they will meet us down at the creek in a little while.

Our creek isn't actually a creek. It's more like a full-sized river, especially this time of year when we've had so much rain. It is also a long hike of rocky and hilly woods to get there. Many times during our walk, my overprotective brother, James, picks me up and lifts me over some rocks or a fallen log. Of all my brothers, I love James the best. He is always taking care of me and watching out for me. He carries me through the woods almost as much as he lets me walk. Since there is no trail from our house to the creek, it can take a lot of time to make the trip. We are always on the lookout for critters and snakes. And if you twist your ankle on one of those big rocks, it will be a slow and painful hike back to the house.

There are three things that make the hike nice on this hot, sunny day: the cool, damp air under the canopy of the trees; our anticipation of swimming in the creek; and the thought that by the time we return home later, we will have a new baby brother or sister.

We finally arrive at the creek and there is a mad dash to remove shoes, stockings, hats, day caps, over-shirts, and suspenders. We leave a trail of clothes and shoes on the grass in the clearing, and we all jump in the creek at the same time, shouting, squealing, and splashing.

The boys splash each other and chase minnows while Susannah and I play in the shallows. She is a good big sister and always treats me like a little baby doll, always taking care of me like I'm her own child. She loves to play with my hair, brushing it and tying ribbons in it. She washes my hair and I lie back in the water to rinse it out. It feels so good to have my hair unbraided and floating freely in the water. As I lay my head back and float, I look up at the canopy of the tall trees with the blue sky behind them. Floating is one of my favorite things in the whole world. Nothing else matters when you are floating in the cool water.

After a little swimming, Susannah and I wash out our clothes and lay them out on the grass in the clearing to dry in the sun. It is so much easier washing our clothes here than in a tub and then hanging them on the line to dry. I tried to help Momma hang clothes one time, but I could barely reach the line, and my arms got tired from holding the clothes up while I tried to pin them. Usually I just stand next to Momma and hand her the clothes one at a time. She keeps the clothespins in a pocket on the front of her apron.

When the slingshot shooters, William and Stephen, finally arrive, they have nothing to show for their skills. As usual, the older boys start picking on them. At first they tease the younger boys about not knowing how to aim. Then the teasing escalates into not knowing how to hunt, and how they would starve if it weren't for their older brothers. When William and Stephen finally get into the water to swim, the older boys start to splash and dunk them. I feel a little sorry for William and Stephen, but I know the teasing is all in fun and someday when they are bigger, they will get the older boys back. William is only eight right now and already almost as tall as Lewis, and Lewis is seventeen.

As the boys are whooping and hollering, I realize we must have lost track of time, because Old Sam comes lumbering out of the woods yelling for us to come eat supper. He carries a basket full of cornbread, butterbeans, and a crock of sweet buttermilk. We ask him how Momma is doing, and he says she is doing fine, but no baby yet. Old Sam places the basket of food down on the grass in the clearing and tells us to remember to bring the basket back home later. We promise him we will remember, and we all sit in the shade of the trees and eat like we have never eaten before. I guess swimming in the creek on a hot day makes us very hungry.

When we finish eating, Susannah and I lie down in the warm sun next to our drying clothes. The older boys take a couple of wooden buckets and head up the creek to hunt for crawdads and frogs. Stephen and William take off in the opposite direction. I don't blame them. They often disappear together and stay away from the bigger boys to avoid getting picked on. They know if they keep to themselves, they will be left alone, and that's the way they like it.

I must have dozed off, because I wake up to the sound of the older boys talking and laughing. They have returned with the two wooden buckets overflowing with crawdads and a couple large frogs. They toss one of the big frogs at Susannah, who squeals and jumps like she is a frog herself. The boys laugh loudly at her and even louder when they scramble in the grass, trying to catch the hopping, croaking frog to put back in the bucket. With all those crawdads and frogs, there will be some good eating tonight if Momma is finished having that baby. If not, we'll just tie the bucket down in the well to stay cool for the night and then cook them tomorrow.

The last time Momma had a baby, it took most of the night and Daddy made us all sleep in the barn. I was only four years old when Hays Jr. was born, but I remember spending the night in the barn because there was a huge screech owl in there that kept us up all night long. It sounded like a woman screaming, and it scared the daylights out of me each and every time it screeched. I curled up in a blanket on the hay, and every time I started to doze off, that owl would screech. I was never happier to see the sun come up than I was the next morning, even though with the rising sun came the loud crowing of our rooster. He was almost as loud as the screech owl, but at least he didn't scare me and make me jump.

"It's starting to get late. I'm going back to the house to see if it is all right for us to come home yet," says Jackson.

I think he suspects he will need to get the barn set up for us to spend the night in, and he wants to get that ready before it gets too dark.

Allen says, "Wait for me. I'll go with you."

"All right," says Lewis. "I'll go down the creek and find Stephen and William and meet you all back here.

My dear James sits down next to me on the grass and stays with me and Susannah.

A little while later, Allen and Jackson return, emerging from the woods, out of breath, shouting, "It's a boy! Momma had a boy!"

Susannah and I look at each other with a little disappointment. We so wanted a little sister to play with. We already have eight brothers. Isn't that enough?

"Let's head back before it gets dark out here," says Allen, gathering clothes and shoes from the grass.

"Where's Lewis?" Jackson asks, looking around. "He went down the creek to find Stephen and William," answers Susannah, sitting on the grass, putting on her shoes.

Suddenly, there is a horrible scream from down the creek, south of us. It is Lewis.

Hurry

In shock and panic, Susannah and I hurry past the boys carrying William and Stephen through the dense woods. We run as fast as we can toward the house. I almost fall at least a dozen times, tripping over logs and rocks, but I keep moving. Getting a scrape or scratch will just be the price I will have to pay if I fall. I have to get home, and I have to get home now.

As we come out of the woods into the field behind our house, I can see the silhouette of Old Sam, chopping firewood in the clearing. I can barely make him out in the dimming light of day, but I know it is him.

"Sam!" I yell. "Come quick. Something happened to William and Stephen!"

I haven't even finished the sentence when Old Sam drops his axe and runs past us toward the woods.

"They're right behind us," I yell after him. "Hurry!"

Susannah keeps running toward the back door of the house, still whimpering. I have to cut her off before she goes inside. I am sure Momma doesn't need to see Susannah in this state after having birthed a baby all day. I run faster to catch up with her and grab the back of her shirt to make her stop.

When she does, I move in front of her to block her way. I point at the log by the back door and breathlessly give her a one-word command: "Sit."

She looks at the log and then back at me like she doesn't understand. I bend over and put my hands on my knees and try to catch my breath. In between gasps for air, I say, "Sit down."

She takes a few steps toward the log and sits down, still whimpering, with her fingers up to her mouth. I hold up my palm to her, like I'm training a dog to stay, and say, "I'll be right back. Don't move."

I go into the house, carefully not letting the back door slam.

It is warm and dark inside. Daddy is on his knees between the big table and the fireplace, placing logs on the fire. He looks up at me, over the table. "Hi, Mary Ann, where are your brothers?"

"Daddy..." I glance at the closed bedroom door sheltering Momma. "Is Momma okay?"

"Momma and the baby are both fine. They are in the bedroom with Bertie. Do you want to see your new brother?"

"Daddy..." I don't really know what to say to him.

Suddenly, Daddy stops moving, holding a log in midair. He squints his eyes at me and asks, "What is it, Mary? What's wrong?"

"Daddy, come outside," is all I can say. I turn and walk back out the door.

Daddy follows me and lets the back door slam behind him as he sees the boys and Old Sam coming out of the woods carrying two lifeless bodies. I've never seen Daddy move so fast.

"What happened?" he asks, panic in his voice, running toward them and awkwardly reaching for both of his sons at the same time.

Lewis responds half through tears. "I don't know, Daddy. We were down at the creek. When I found them, they were both in the water, not breathing. I think they're dead, Daddy."

As they lay the bodies of an eight-year-old boy and a ten-year-old boy on the red dirt at my daddy's feet, the only place to stay out of the way is next to Susannah on the log. I sit down next to her and take her shaking hand in mine.

I watch Daddy and Old Sam kneel on the ground next to William and Stephen.

When I look at Old Sam, I realize we forgot to bring back the picnic basket.

The Funeral

The next morning, I wake to the sound of our rooster crowing. It isn't quite light outside yet, but I know someone will be awake in the house.

I lie still and listen for any sound, but the house seems unusually quiet. Under the bedroom door, I can see the glow of the fireplace in the next room, and I can smell biscuits and gravy cooking, so I know someone is already up. I look next to me and in the dim light I see a lump that is Susannah under the quilt. I can hear her breathing softly. She's still asleep.

I look at the other beds. They are empty. Timothy and Hays Jr. stayed the night at Reverend and Mrs. Jones's house, and William and Stephen are not here. My heart feels like it stops cold and I gasp for air and feel tears well up. I rub my eyes, with my fists clenched into little balls, and wipe the tears away. Maybe it's all just a bad dream.

I wonder why Bertie hasn't awakened us as I slowly push the quilt off my legs and gently crawl out of bed, careful to not wake Susannah. I glance at the empty beds that belong to my brothers and feel a pain in my chest I've never felt before. I tiptoe out of the room and quietly close the door behind me. Our main room is empty, with only the fireplace burning brightly. There are four chairs, a large table that we eat on surrounded by four more chairs, and two smaller tables that hold candles. Next to the fireplace are pots and pans and a giant stack of firewood. A cast-iron pot hangs from the hook over the fire and bubbles with gravy cooking for our breakfast. Biscuits are cooling on the big table. From the mantle hangs drying stockings and one of Daddy's shirts, and on top of the mantle sits his pipe and rifle. I hear someone come in the back door, but decide to peek into the next room to check on Momma and the baby before saying good morning to anyone else.

I crack open the door to Momma's room and see her sitting up in bed holding the new baby. It is a very small room, packed with two huge chests of drawers, a feather bed with a table next to it, and a cradle for the new baby. On the table next to the bed, there is a candle burning that fills the room with a soft, flickering light. The glow shines on top of the baby's head. I look next to Momma and around the room, but Daddy isn't here. He must have already gotten up.

"Hi, Momma," I whisper.

"Hi, sweet girl." She smiles. She pats the top of the quilt with her free hand. "Come on in here and meet your new baby brother."

I walk over to the edge of the bed and stand on my tiptoes, but all I can see is the top of his little head of dark hair. Momma leans over so I can get a better look at him. He is bundled up in a blanket with only his head and one little arm showing. I giggle because his tiny hand looks a little wrinkled, like when you've stayed in the water too long. His fingers are long and he scrunches them into a fist. I reach out and touch his black hair, which feels as soft as silk. He opens his little eyes when I touch him and spread his wrinkled fingers wide. I smile and look up at Momma.

"He's so little," I whisper.

"Yes, I think he was born a little early," says Momma softly as she gazes lovingly at the baby. "I wasn't expecting him for a few more weeks."

"What did you name him?" I ask, gently patting the top of his head.

"Well, I haven't named him yet. What do you think his name should be?" Momma asks, looking at me. I hesitate, wondering if anyone has told Momma about Stephen and William. I feel an ache in the pit of my stomach and think for a moment that I may throw up. Something inside tells me that if this baby wasn't born yesterday, then we would not have been down at the creek, and William and Stephen would still be alive. If this baby took the lives of two others, then he must be very important indeed. He should have a name to mark the day he was born. Then I think, if you put Stephen and William together, you get Stellam or Willsen.

"I think we should call him Wilson," I blurt out, but I don't say, "after William and Stephen."

She looks down at the baby and her face changes to a sad expression. I freeze, hoping Momma knows what happened. If she doesn't, she probably wouldn't look this unhappy. I hope I didn't make her sad. I don't move. I don't breathe.

After a moment, she looks up, gives me a sad kind of smile, and slowly says, "I think Wilson is a fine name. We'll call him Wilson."

She looks down at the baby. "Wilson," she says to him.

Then she looks back at me. "You should run along now and get dressed and eat some breakfast. Reverend and Mrs. Jones are going to be here later today, so we can have a funeral for your brothers on top of the hill."

I can tell she is fighting back tears, trying to not cry, but I feel a big relief that she knows about William and Stephen, and I don't have to be the one to tell her. I don't know what she means by a funeral, but I figure I will find out in good time.

I rise onto my tiptoes, kiss the top of the baby's head, and whisper, "Buh-bye, Wilson."

I quietly leave the room, and as I close the door, I can hear Momma crying. I stand on the other side of the closed door for a few minutes and listen to her. I pout and wipe away my own tears. My heart is aching for my brothers. It is now breaking into little tiny pieces for my momma.

* * *

Later that afternoon, Momma and Daddy, my brothers, and Susannah and I walk to the top of the hill at the back of our land. It is a warm, humid day, with big gray storm clouds hanging in the distance. The wind gusts once in a while, rustling the leaves up in the trees. I don't know how long this funeral is going to take, but I hope we finish before the rain comes. It looks like it's going to be a stormy evening.

Reverend and Mrs. Jones are already at the top of the hill waiting for us. There are some other neighbors there as well. Mr. and Mrs. Pace, Mr. and Mrs. Calhoun, and Mr. and Mrs. Carpenter are all there, along with some of their children I know from school. Bertie does not come with us. She stays at the house to take care of baby Wilson. Old Sam is here. He brought a chair from the house for Momma to sit on. I watch him carefully place it on the grass for Momma then move to the back of the small crowd. I think he looks older than he did yesterday.

In front of a row of big pine trees, there are two fresh mounds of red dirt covering graves that contain my brothers. My first thought at the sight of the graves is that the boys won't be able to breathe down there, and then I remember they aren't breathing anymore. I wonder how long one can go without breathing. I hold my breath, but after a minute, I give up and exhale.

I don't know anything about burying anyone. The only deaths I have ever seen are chickens and deer and such. We don't bury those; they are supper. I'm glad we don't eat folks.

There is a wooden cross, made of two pieces of wood held together with twine, at the head of each grave. One has the initials WR carved on it, and one has the initials SR. I look around at the people, wondering who made the crosses. As I glance at Old Sam, he puts his head down and wipes away a tear. I know at that very second that it was he who spent the entire night burying the boys and making the crosses. He looks so sad and so tired. I wish I could go give him a hug right now, but that doesn't seem the appropriate thing to do, so I stand next to Momma's chair.

I look up at Daddy and see that he looks tired, too. I glance down at his hand resting on Momma's shoulder and see that his fingernails are caked with red dirt. I look up at him and think he must have stayed out here with Old Sam all night burying my brothers. That's why he was not with Momma this morning. He did not go to bed.

Momma tries not to cry, but I hear a sob escape from her. Daddy stands tall next to her, his face like a stone as he rubs her shoulder. My brothers stand behind Momma and Daddy, wearing their Sunday best, with their hands folded. Susannah sits on the ground in front of Momma, with no expression on her face. She is staring straight ahead at the mounds of dirt, but she doesn't seem to be looking at them.

My friend from school, Rice Carpenter, moves over and stands next to me. He doesn't say anything, but I can see out of the corner of my eye that he's looking at me. He bumps my hand with his, but I just ignore him. I'm sure now is not the time to play games.

I listen closely to Reverend Jones to see if I can learn something, anything, to help make sense of what happened.

Reverend Jones starts the funeral by saying, "Dear friends and family, we are here to mourn the lives of these two young boys, William Rodgers and Stephen Rodgers."

Momma sobs.

"We are also here to celebrate the lives of

these two young boys. For the last eight and ten years, our task as family and friends has been to witness their lives. Life is worth nothing if there is no one to notice it and acknowledge it. We are here to notice them, to acknowledge them, and to be their witnesses. We don't know if life will be very long, or, as in the case of William and Stephen, painfully short. But it is not ours to question God's will, only to witness His miracle of life."

Reverend Jones's voice changes to a softer tone. "Our job now," —he emphasizes *now* —"is to honor their memories. As with the loss of any loved one, we only have memories to cling to. We have the memory of their smile, their laughter, the way they loved, the way they cried. We need to hang on to those memories and help each other to not forget." He changes his voice again to a happier tone and says that through our sorrow, we need to give thanks and praise to the Lord that we will see Stephen and William again someday in Heaven. Somebody says, "Hallelujah." I look in the direction of the voice but can't tell who said it.

Reverend Jones then reads out of the Bible for a while, and when he finishes, one of the ladies from church sings a song. Reverend Jones ends the funeral with a prayer and everyone says, "Amen."

The funeral is over, and I still don't understand any of it.

Momma slowly stands up and walks over to the graves. She places some daisies on each of the graves, right in front of the crosses. The ladies at the funeral shed their own tears as they hug Momma and tell her they are so sorry and will come by soon to see the new baby. The men at the funeral sadly shake Daddy's hand and pat my brothers on their shoulders. The sky is starting to darken with rain clouds. Everyone quickly says their goodbyes and hurries to get home before the rain starts.

My family stays for a little while after everyone leaves. But soon, the wind starts to pick up and the sky becomes darker and we know we need to head back. Daddy and Old Sam help Momma back down the hill toward the house.

Susannah walks ahead of us like she is in a daze. I don't understand why she has suddenly become so sullen. I run to catch up with her. While I'm walking next to her, looking up at her, trying to get her attention, James comes up beside me and takes my hand. I look up at him and he smiles back down at me. James and I, hand in hand, slow down and let Susannah walk by herself.

When we finally get back to the house, just missing the downpour by minutes, I help Bertie set the table for supper. James fixes me a plate and pours me a cup of buttermilk. We eat a yummy supper of warmed-up greens and cornbread that the neighbor ladies brought over for us. Bertie places the food on the table with one hand, while holding baby Wilson with the other. Momma has gone back to bed for the night. As I eat, I glance at Momma's closed bedroom door, wondering if she is all right.

After supper, I crawl into my own bed and silently cry into my pillow for a long time. It has been the saddest day I have ever known, except for yesterday.

As I listen to the pitter-patter of the rain on

the roof, I look over at the empty bed that used to belong to William and Stephen. I wonder if I will ever feel happy again. Eventually, sleep comes.

The New House

In the weeks following the funeral, Daddy isn't around very much. When I ask where Daddy is, Momma tells me that the government made some kind of deal with the Indians and bought a lot of land from them. She says a government man called a surveyor is going to come around and map the new government land, and then sell off sections for a really good price. Momma tells me Daddy has gone to look for some flat and fertile farmland before the surveyor man arrives, so he can stake his claim and be ready to buy it the moment it is for sale.

I sit on a wooden stool next to the table, listening to the story while watching Momma knead some dough on the flour-covered wooden table.

"So the Indians are gone now?" I ask her.

"Well, not all of them, but most have gone."

"What's Daddy going to do with the land when he buys it?"

"Eventually we are going to pack all of our things in the wagon and go live there."

She punches the top of the dough and flips it over on the table.

"Are there still going to be Indians living there?" I ask cautiously.

"No, no. They have a new place to live called Oklahoma. There won't be any Indians when we go there."

I am happy about that.

After I think about it for a moment, I ask her, "But Momma, how can we live there with no house?" Momma starts wiping her hands with a damp cloth to get rid of the flour.

"Your daddy has already found some good, flat land, and has been there with Old Sam and your brothers for the last few weeks building our new house. It won't have a dirt floor like the house we have now. Daddy is putting in a wood floor and a loft for sleeping."

"You mean like the loft in the barn?"

"Yes, just like in the barn, but no screech owl." Momma reaches over and tickles my stomach.

I giggle as I push her hand away. "Can we go see the new house now?"

"Maybe Daddy will take you after he comes home. He said he would be home in a few days so we should see him anytime now."

I am so very excited to move into our new house with a real wood floor and a loft for sleeping, but we don't end up moving for a very long time. The current crops are harvested and new ones are planted before the surveyor man even shows up. By the time Daddy has harvested those crops, the surveying is finally done and Daddy buys eighty acres from the government, including the land our new house is built on. He also buys a hundred and sixty acres next to it from Mr. Calhoun.

Mr. Calhoun purchased land from the government, too, but then he had second thoughts and decided he would rather move closer to town and start a leather tannery. He is excited about making boots and shoes for the folks in the community, so he sells his land to Daddy.

By the time we pack all of our things and move into our new house, Momma is ready to give birth again. I am a little anxious and uneasy about the whole process after what happened when Wilson was born, but everything goes smoothly and she gives birth to yet another boy. She names him John. John is a sweet little baby with the usual Rodgers' dark hair and blue eyes. Even though he is the cutest little boy ever, I sure wish he were a girl.

After we get settled into our new house, Daddy buys two more slaves to help with the new land. At the end of the year, Daddy says they have cleared and cultivated sixty-five acres. Counting my older brothers, my daddy, Old Sam, and the two new slaves, all the work of clearing, planting, and harvesting is done by only eight men, two oxen, and a lot of backbreaking labor. I don't see Daddy much, and realize I haven't really seen him a whole lot the past couple years, and I wish for the days when Daddy was around more.

I guess cotton is like gold around here, and even though Daddy says cotton prices have fallen a bit recently, he is still doing very, very well. Tonight, after I crawl in bed, I overhear Daddy in the other room telling Momma that he sold eleven bales of cotton at seventy dollars per bale. I do a quick calculation with the math skills I learned at school, and can only think one thing—we must be rich.

In 1841, Daddy has a total of four hundred acres after he bought a hundred and sixty more from a couple of men in the community. He clears and plows land and rotates his crops and uses animal manure to fertilize them to get even bigger harvests. He works every day from sunup until sundown. He buys more slaves to help in the fields, and more chickens, hogs, and cows to help feed the slaves. The slaves build pens for the hogs, roosts for the chickens, and a pretty large log home for themselves. Momma says that Daddy is going to buy some sheep in the spring, and she will teach me and Susannah how to spin wool and work the new loom that Old Sam is building. She is going to show us how to dye the wool with berries and tree bark to make new clothes for our family.

It will be nice to have soft wool clothes instead of linen clothes made from flax. It takes a lot of muscle to separate the flax fibers from the plants and make material out of it. I wish we could wear cotton clothes but cotton is our cash crop. We make more money selling it than we ever would wearing it. But that's all right. Very soon we will have fancy new wool clothes.

It all seems like a good plan at the time, but children don't stay children forever. My older brothers and sister are starting to make plans for themselves. After the harvest of '41, my oldest brother, Lewis, announces he is getting married to a neighbor girl and moving to Texas with her family. This is going to cut down on Daddy's labor force. It is also going to leave a big hole in our family. Lewis is the oldest of the children and is just about Daddy's right hand. He is pretty much the overseer of the farm, and I don't know who will step into his shoes.

Those are some big shoes to fill.

If my heart isn't already aching enough at the thought of Lewis moving away, Susannah announces that she too is going to marry. She is madly in love with a neighbor boy, Elijah Chatham. I have always liked Elijah, but I wish he and Susannah would just live with us instead of moving into their own home. At least she is not moving to Texas like Lewis, thank goodness. But still, I can't imagine living in the house without Susannah. How can I survive with no sister? I am losing the one person I have spent every day and every night with for twelve years. She is my best friend and we share everything. I will be left in the house with nothing but brothers. I am happy for Susannah, but sad for myself.

Susannah wants her wedding to be first, so she plans to have her wedding in January, before Lewis's April wedding. So within a few short months, we all put on our fanciest clothes and meet at the church.

Susannah looks like a princess, dressed in her new ivory-colored wool dress with a beautiful lace veil trailing down her back. As she looks at Elijah, I realize I have never seen her look so happy. She is positively beaming.

Reverend Jones performs a charming ceremony and all the ladies from the community show up in their fanciest hats and bring their best dishes. We have a grand celebration with lots of food and lots of music, and I dare say, lots of sneaking outside by the men to get a little taste of moonshine.

I spend the entire afternoon sitting under a big pine tree talking with Rice, the boy from school.

He is the same age as me and we've been friends since we were little. He is almost six foot tall now, with sandy blonde hair and twinkling blue eyes the color of the sky. He is kind and handsome and has the best manners, but the most attractive thing about him is his smile. He has teeth as white as pearls and his dazzling smile brightens up every room. Every time he looks at me, I feel myself blush. Every time he smiles at me, I get butterflies in my stomach.

Rice and his family live right down the road from us, so we see each other often. We go to school together every day. And when we aren't at school, we are running into each other between our family homes. I think Rice is the cutest and nicest boy around, and I hope someday he will be my boyfriend. Today, for a brief moment, I even let myself dream that we might have a wedding as grand as Susannah's.

Daddy throws quite a gala. He says nothing is too good for his first-born daughter, and he invites family and friends from around the county and across the state. Susannah is his first child to be married, and I have the feeling Daddy has been planning this day for eighteen years.

Guests are arriving from as far away as Alabama and Tennessee, two and three days in advance of the wedding, and Daddy stops all of the work on the farm to have the slaves put up makeshift houses and tents for the adults to sleep in. Some of the children sleep in the barn, and some sleep in the wagons they arrived in. Some of the fancier folk who can afford it stay at the boarding house in Marion or the hotel down in Meridian, but most of the guests stay with us on Daddy's land.

For days, Bertie cooks massive amounts of food, and I think I might just explode from eating so much. The gathering at our house is bigger and better than the wedding itself, if that is even possible. And when the wedding celebration is over, it takes most of them two or three days to pack up and leave. It is so much fun seeing relatives I never even knew existed, and very sad saying goodbye to them all.

A few months later, on an early April morning, my brother Lewis and his girl, Nancy, are married in the same church by the same reverend with the same neighbors in attendance, but there just isn't the same air of gaiety as at Susannah's wedding. Lewis and Nancy have all of their meager possessions packed in a wagon outside the church door and are ready to set out on their great adventure right after the ceremony. Since Daddy cannot throw them a big wedding like he did for Susannah, he gives them an ox for a wedding gift. They already have it hooked up to their wagon in preparation to leave immediately.

We exchange tearful hugs and goodbyes, knowing that we will probably never see each other again. I haven't felt pain and emptiness like this since the day we buried my brothers on the hill six years ago. Saying goodbye is the hardest thing in the whole world.

But again, as with the funeral, my friend Rice is there to ease my sadness. After Lewis's wedding, Daddy allows Rice to walk me home from church, and we spend the afternoon laughing, talking, and flirting in the warm April sunshine.

In '42, Susannah gives birth to the first grandchild in the family. My nephew is a fine-looking boy with dark hair and blue eyes, just like his mother. She names him James Monroe Chatham after our brother, James. He immediately becomes the light of my days, and I have never loved a little boy so much in my life.

With all the little ones in my family, I have seen newborns many times, but never one with such a look of maturity in his eyes. Those blue eyes look around the room like they know everyone and everything. He is an amazing and smart little boy. I love to play with him every chance I get, for nothing more than to just make him smile. I spend hours and hours holding and rocking him and singing songs to him. As he grows, he crawls before every other baby I have ever known, and walks and talks before all of them, too. He is an exceptional boy, and I am deeply, head over heels in love with him.

Right after the Christmas season, my brother Allen announces his plans to marry Judith McGehee. They have a small, quiet ceremony at the church, and Allen immediately moves out of our home to live with his new bride. They move up to Carroll County, which is a whole day away by wagon. I know the moment they leave that I will rarely see Allen again.

Allen is kind and loving, and has always been the quiet one of the boys. He seldom says a word unless you directly ask him a question. You don't even know he is in the room unless you trip over him. I guess growing up in the shadow of Lewis, who is Mr. Take Charge, Allen didn't need to step up very often, if ever, and he slid into that role without complaint.

The day after Allen's wedding, I am feeling so sad about him moving away. I sit on the wooden steps of our front porch in the sunshine, with my chin in my hands, brooding over losing yet another brother. I move pebbles in the dirt with my foot as I pout and sulk. My protective brother, James, comes out of the house and plops down beside me.

"What's wrong?" he asks.

"I was just thinking that I don't like it when one of you boys starts liking a girl. You always marry her and move away, and I don't like to say goodbye. It's not that I mind change so much. I just don't like to lose one of you."

James is quiet for a moment then says, "But I thought you were tired of having so many brothers around."

"Well, yeah, I guess, but I still like to have my family all in one place."

James agrees with me and adds, "Well, in a short time, you'll have a new baby brother to replace Allen."

My mouth falls open as I spin my head and look at him with disbelief. James points at me and laughs at my expression as he gets up and takes off across the yard. Momma is expecting another child? How did I not see it?

A couple months later, Momma gives birth again. But James's prediction isn't correct. This one isn't a boy. Momma has a girl! Elizabeth is the most beautiful little girl in the whole world. We spoil her with trinkets and toys and the best clothes made from the prettiest cloth. I am so elated to finally have a little sister; I don't think I will ever get the smile off my face. I make her a little bonnet with white lace trim, and I embroider pink flowers all over it. I brush her soft hair and tie ribbons in her dark brown locks, just like Susannah used to do with my hair. Elizabeth has the same blue eyes as the rest of the family. She is so cute, and I finally have the little sister I have been praying for for twelve years.

On days I don't have school, while Momma works in the garden or goes out to chase the pigs out of the chicken feed, I mind baby Elizabeth. I also have three-year-old John and six-year-old Wilson under my feet. Momma teaches me to lift up the end of the bedpost or the table leg and put the edge of John's baby dress underneath it. That way he can't get too close to the fireplace or get into trouble while no one is looking. She also tells me to put honey on his hands and give him a feather to play with. That will keep him busy for so long that we can actually get some chores done around the house, and it is hilarious to watch.

Between babies, the garden, the chickens and cows, making soap and candles, churning butter, spinning and dyeing wool, shucking corn to take to the mill, and attending school daily, I fall into bed every night completely exhausted. I wonder how Momma and Bertie keep going day after day. They sit by the firelight every night, mending clothes or sewing quilts long after I and the other children have gone to bed, yet they wake before us every morning without fail.

In 1843, Susannah gives birth to her second child, Sarah, and in 1844, her third, John Hays, who is named after our brother, John, and our daddy, Hays. In October of the same year, Momma gives birth to another girl, Martha Jane.

I can tell from the very day she is born that Martha Jane is going to be a spoiled little princess. Daddy's farm is doing so well that he actually slows down and takes time to spend with the baby girl. I have never seen him do that before. He was always working day and night to make the farm successful, but for some reason, this child is different, and Daddy goes out of his way to dote on Martha Jane.

She is certainly growing up differently than the rest of us did. She has a drawer full of clothes and a box full of toys. I remember when Susannah and I only had one dress apiece. Martha Jane has two parents to take care of her instead of just one. She also has more slaves around to cook and clean for her than any of us ever did. She doesn't have near the amount of chores the rest of us had. She is, in a word, spoiled.

We receive word that Lewis's wife has given him two sons out in Texas, and Allen's wife is expecting their first. Susannah also gives birth. Her fourth child is a pretty little girl she names Mary, after me. Our family is growing by leaps and bounds, and it looks like there's no end in sight.

When I am not doing chores or watching the little ones, I spend more and more time with Rice. We spend many lazy afternoons down by the creek, and many romantic evenings chasing fireflies and walking hand in hand through the fields in the moonlight.

This afternoon by the creek, I am lying in the

sun in the clearing when I suddenly feel a shadow cross my face. When I open my eyes, Rice is lying next to me on the grass with his head above me, looking down into my face. When he sees me open my eyes, he gives me that gorgeous smile of his that melts my heart.

"You're in my sun," I tease.

"You don't need any sun. You're beautiful just the way you are," he says.

He reaches up and gently pushes the hair from my temple. I feel butterflies in my stomach at his touch. Then he slowly comes closer and gently kisses me right on the mouth. Until this point, our relationship has been only innocent flirtation. This changes everything.

After the lingering kiss, he lifts his head and opens his eyes. I try to catch my breath and make my head stop spinning. He smiles at me again. That is it. One little kiss and that unbelievable smile and I admit to myself that I am madly in love with this handsome boy.

"I have a secret," he teases.

"What?"

He reaches in his shirt pocket, pulls out something, and holds it up in front of my face. I narrow my eyes to bring it into focus. Between his index finger and his thumb is a gold ring.

"Your daddy says since you are eighteen now, I can give this to you."

His smile is bigger and brighter than I've ever seen it.

I don't say anything. For the first time in my life, I'm stunned into silence. Is he asking me to marry him? My head is spinning. My heart is beating out of my chest.

"Well? Will you marry me?" He grins.

I am shouting *"Yes"* inside my head, but I think it will be more fun to play with him.

"I don't know," I answer. "What's in it for me?" For a moment he looks disheartened, and I can't stand to see that uneasy look on his face.

"I'm just kidding, Rice. Of course I will marry you!"

I sit up and hug him. He slips the ring onto my finger and kisses me again, but with more passion this time. Oh, my head is spinning again. And these butterflies are flying faster and faster. In my mind, I play the words over and over again— Mrs. Rice Carpenter.

1847

On a crisp fall morning, I step into my beautiful wedding dress made by my beloved Bertie. It is ivory-colored wool with a high lace collar and low-pointed waist. She embroidered gorgeous pink roses with green leaves all over it. It also has rows of chain-stitch embroidery at the neck and the ends of the bell-shaped sleeves. Momma and Bertie spend what seems like hours closing up the back, buttoning dozens of the tiniest buttons. Underneath, there is a new corset, pantaloons, and the finest crinolines.

Just before we leave to go to the church, Momma braids my hair and tucks it into the most fabulous veil I've ever seen. It looks like a sheer nightcap, but under the gathers in the back, it has a sheer train attached that hangs down to my waist. Bertie embroidered pink roses all over that as well. She has also made me stockings and slippers with the same pink rose embroidery. Bertie's sewing talents are unsurpassed. I feel like a princess.

Rice and I are to be married in the same church as all the other members of my family. On the way to the church, I notice the trees are just beginning to drop their leaves and the air is enchanting and delicious.

I am nervous as I enter the back of the church with Daddy by my side, and I stare down at my bouquet of white daisies, for if I look up, I may faint. But when I finally do look up, I see Rice in his handsome wedding attire waiting for me at the front of the church, and all of my anxieties evaporate. He looks like a handsome prince in his black waistcoat with short tails, and his smile lights up the entire room and makes everything and everyone disappear. All I see is him and that smile.

I have never seen Rice dressed up before, and he is amazingly and devastatingly handsome with that sandy blonde hair. From the moment I enter the door, we can't take our eyes off each other. I am so entranced with the sight of him and the thought of becoming his wife that I don't even hear a word the reverend says during the ceremony. We finally say, "I do," and kiss each other on the lips right there in front of everyone. I am blissfully happy.

When we turn around to leave the altar, I notice Susannah. She is sitting in the front pew with Momma and Daddy, looking like a giant watermelon in a mint-green dress and bonnet. I almost laugh out loud when I see her, but quickly compose myself with the thought of how uncomfortable she must be. After giving birth to her daughter, Mary, last year, she is now as big as a house with her fifth child. I can just imagine how she feels sitting on that hard wooden pew.

I know that as a good and faithful wife, my duty is to have children, especially sons to work the farm, but I hope Rice and I can enjoy being newlyweds for a long, long time. I love children, but I am in no hurry to start having them, especially five children in six years like Susannah. Good grief.

Following our wedding ceremony, we have a great celebration. Again, Daddy spares no expense in throwing the best party in town. Relatives and guests have been flooding the house for a week. The ladies from the community bring delicious casseroles, and Rice's dad butchered a hog to supply us with the biggest summer ham I have ever seen. As the evening lingers on and the sun begins to set, the men play fiddle, harp, and a washboard drum. We talk and laugh and eat and dance until very late in the evening.

When Rice and I finally leave in his wagon, I am both very sad the party is over and very excited to begin my new life with my new husband. I am quietly lost in thought.

Finally, Rice breaks the silence. "Are you all right?"

A little startled by the question, yet understanding why he asked it, I say, "Yes, of course, I'm just taking it all in. I'm a little sad the party is over." I pout and entwine my arms around his.

"Well, I have a surprise for you. It will cheer you up," Rice says as he snaps the reins to make the horse move faster.

"What kind of surprise?"

"You'll have to wait and see, Mrs. Carpenter," he teases.

"Mrs. Carpenter. I like the sound of that." I grin, totally forgetting about the surprise.

About halfway to Daddy's house, Rice turns off the road. We pull up in front of a small log home on what I think is Daddy's land, but I have never seen this home before. On the porch are torches that I know someone recently lit because they are not burned down very far. The front of the house has two windows, and I can see through the glass that there is an inviting fire inside.

"What is this?" I ask as he stops in front of the house.

Rice leans over, puts his arm around my shoulder, and stares at the house. I look at him and back at the house, and then back at him, waiting for an answer.

He says, "Your daddy gave us this land as a wedding gift, and the home you are looking at is the home I've been building for us for the last month. Do you like it?"

"Like it? It's beautiful. I wondered where you've been disappearing to for the last couple weeks. I can't believe you have done this. Rice, it's so beautiful." I am in awe of the house and the man.

"Well, there isn't much in it yet," he says, as he climbs down from the wagon and walks around to my side. He stops next to me and looks up at me. "But I promise I will work day and night to fill it with furniture, if you will work day and night to fill it with children and love."

He puts his hands around my waist and lifts me out of the wagon. As he gently sets me on the ground, he bends his head down and kisses me. Butterflies. He is such an incredible man; my heart skips a beat at his tenderness. After our kiss, I stand there and stare at the beautiful home, amazed that it is ours. Rice lifts me in his arms and carries me over the threshold.

* * *

We quickly start filling our house and turning it into a home. Rice builds a table and chairs, and then surprises me with the most beautiful hand-carved four-poster bed. I spend many hours spinning flax to make the covering for our mattress, and many sneezing hours filling the mattress with down and feathers. I also make some new sheets for our new bed, which is fairly easy, and then I make Rice two new linen shirts, which is a little more complicated. Rice installs an exquisitely carved mantle over our fireplace and lovely shutters on the windows. We plant a modest vegetable garden, buy some chickens and sheep, and borrow Daddy's oxen to plow the field for cotton, corn, and flax. Rice builds an outdoor kitchen to cook in during the hot summer months, and I spend many hours out there canning berries and fruit.

In between all the work, we spend romantic hours down at the creek and walking through the fields. We sometimes laze in our cozy bed into the late morning hours, and spend warm afternoons sitting on the front porch planning our future.

This evening, Rice and his brother, Hilliard, are sitting on the porch, excitedly talking up a storm.

"What in the world are you boys so excited about tonight?" I ask.

"We are planning your new barn," Hilliard answers.

"A barn? Really, Rice? We're going to have a barn?"

"Well, I just bought a new horse today, and

the poor thing needs a place to live, don't you think?"

"We already have a horse and he lives in the pasture just fine. We don't need a barn for a horse. What are you two really up to?" I sit in a chair beside Rice.

"Truthfully, Hilliard and I just bought a new cotton gin and need a place to put it. If we do this right, we could be rich very soon," Rice says.

Oh, my goodness. A cotton gin? Rich? I don't know what to think, but if Rice wants to run a cotton gin and be rich, I am all for that.

Rice begins gathering lumber and hardware and clears the land to build the barn. Hilliard, Daddy, my brother James, and half of the neighbor men are all on our land, having a big barn-raising out in the field behind our house. I have never actually seen anyone put up a barn before, and I am pleasantly surprised and amazed at how fast it goes up if you have enough people working on it. It takes the men about a week to finish it. Bertie comes over to help and she and I cook more food in that week than I have cooked in the whole time Rice and I have been married.

* * *

As our house is coming along nicely, we decide it is time to invite our first guests. We invite Rice's sister Betsy and her husband, Gray, over for an evening of dining and playing cards. I light the candles and Rice lights our fancy new oil lamp. The house looks warm and cozy. It smells of chicken with rosemary spice roasting in the pot over the fireplace. It feels like a home filled with unlimited amounts of love.

Betsy is the eldest of Rice's siblings. She and Gray Sanderford have been married for almost twenty years. They got married about the time Rice was born, so Rice did not grow up with her, but they are still as close as siblings can be. I am not only excited to show off our home to her, but also curious as to any advice she can give me to make it even better.

When Betsy and Gray arrive, we dine on a scrumptious supper of roasted chicken, greens, and squash. After supper, Rice takes Gray outside to show off the new barn, while Betsy and I clear the dishes from the table and discuss married life and children.

Betsy is a beautiful woman, with the same sandy blonde hair, blue eyes, and dazzling smile as her brother. If she is any indication of what Rice will resemble twenty years from now, I am a lucky woman. Betsy and Gray have four older girls— Harriet, Martha, Bethanie, and Pernecia—followed by two younger boys, John and Elisha. All of them look just like Betsy. Apparently, the Carpenter blood is very strong.

Betsy is now pregnant with her seventh child. She tells me she hopes this one will be a boy also, because Gray sure could use the help around the farm. Betsy goes on and on about what a blessing the children are, and how grateful she is that even though Harriet and Martha are old enough, at eighteen and sixteen, to be married, they are still home with her. Betsy is a good and devoted mother, and she is as beautiful inside as she is on the outside. Gray is a lucky man to find such a good wife.

When Betsy and I finish washing the dishes, we sit back down at the table with our cups of tea. Betsy is telling me all the latest news about her children. Thanie, short for Bethanie, is being courted by some young boy from the Snowden family. She's only fourteen, and Gray is about ready to chase that boy out of town with a gun if he doesn't stop coming around. Betsy laughs as she tells me the story, and I get the feeling she likes the boy, even if Gray doesn't.

As she tells her story, I reach down and tug on my corset. With a quizzical look, Betsy asks what I am doing. I tell her I'm not sure why, but my corset is so tight around the top, it is making my breasts ache.

Betsy asks, "Were your breasts aching this morning before you put on your corset?"

"Well, now that you mention it, they have been aching for a week."

Betsy giggles and puts her hand up to her lips. She stares at me with that huge Carpenter smile on her face, her eyes twinkling in the candlelight.

"What is so funny?" I ask, looking at her sideways.

"I believe you, my dear Mary, are with child!" She giggles.

I am stunned by the revelation and her candidness and start to giggle also.

As if on cue, the men enter the back door

right at that moment. Betsy and I both stop in mid-giggle and look at them. We must have the funniest expressions on our faces, because both men freeze like statues.

"Well, we should be going now," says Betsy, as she quickly rises to her feet, grabs her bonnet and pulls her husband to the front door in one move. "It's getting late." She giggles again. "Thank you for a lovely supper. We'll see you both at church on Sunday."

Gray, confused, looks at Rice, nods, and then tips his hat to me.

"Er, uh, good evening, all," he says. And they are gone.

Rice asks, "What was that all about? Why was my sister acting so funny? I thought we were going to play cards."

I hesitate to answer, but I am sure Betsy is right. I have already suspected it myself.

"Well?" he asks again while taking off his jacket and hanging it on the hook near the door.

I stand up to get his attention, straight and tall and with my hands folded together at my waist like an old school teacher. I clear my throat.

"Rice," I begin, "if Betsy is right, I believe you're going to be a father."

He stops moving. His arms, having just hung up his jacket, freeze in midair. I wait. After a moment, he turns to me with no expression on his face, and slowly lowers his arms to his sides.

"Did you hear me, Rice?" I ask cautiously. "I think I am with child."

Slowly, like molasses dripping in the cold, he

starts to grin. It turns into the biggest smile I have ever seen on his face. He walks over, wraps his arms around me, picks me up, and spins me around in a circle. When he puts me back on the floor, he leans over and kisses me tenderly. Butterflies.

"I reckon I ought to get busy building a cradle," he says softly through his grin. "Do you know when?"

"I've suspected for some time, so close to Christmas, I think."

Rice holds me close, his arms still around my waist, with mine around his neck. He whispers in my ear, "We are going to be a very, very happy family. I love you, Mary Ann Carpenter."

"I love you, too, Rice Carpenter."

It warms my heart to see him so happy. I slowly take his hands from my waist and place them on my stomach. He smiles that smile.

Betsy

Rice and I excitedly prepare for our first child. He builds a handsome cradle and carves toys from wood. I spend most evenings in front of the fireplace, sewing baby gowns and patching together a small baby quilt. The time we used to spend romancing each other is now spent preparing for the arrival of our baby, but we don't mind the interruption.

A fall morning, right before the harvest, Betsy's daughter, Martha, comes knocking on our door. She is only sixteen, but is amazingly mature. Except for the age difference, she and Betsy could be twins. I think in passing that Martha will make a good wife someday and probably produce very pretty babies. I have seen her on occasion in the company of my brother, James, but I don't think she has a beau.

"Hi, Aunt Mary." She smiles warmly. She has that Carpenter smile that lights up every room.

"Hello there, Martha, what can I do for you?" I push the front door open and step aside to let her come in.

As she steps into the house, she says, "Momma asked me to come tell you she went to her birthing bed. She said you'd want to know."

"Oh, how exciting! Please tell your mother I'm so happy for her. I will make a big pot of stew and bring it by the house later this afternoon for your daddy and the children to have for supper. Hopefully the labor will go quickly and she will have delivered by the time I get there," I ramble, excited for the arrival of a new baby in the family.

After Martha leaves, I head out to the garden and pick some vegetables for the stew. I draw a big bucket of water from the well and light the fireplace. After putting the vegetables, water, spices, and some leftover chicken from last night's supper into the iron pot, I hang it on the handle above the fire, put the lid on, and let it simmer. The stew cooks for a couple hours and smells delicious, filling the house with the most tantalizing aroma. Apparently I am hungry, but I decide to wait until I get to Betsy's house to eat. It will be nice to sit down and eat with her family, hopefully with the new baby present.

When the pot cools, I call for Rice to hitch up the horse to the wagon. He pulls the wagon up to the front of the house, and I load the pot of stew into the back. I run inside to grab my bonnet and Rice follows me to get his jacket. We are almost ready to leave when Gray unexpectedly pulls up in front of the house and knocks on the door.

Before I can ask if Betsy had a boy or a girl, he blurts out, "She's dead."

"What?!" I take a step back.

"She's dead. She had a boy and died in the birthing bed. My beautiful Betsy is dead."

I stand frozen in shock as Rice, who has heard the conversation from the other room, comes up next to me. Neither of us knows what to say. I look from Rice to Gray and back again. I don't know who to feel worse for, Gray, who has lost his wife, or Rice, who has lost his sister. We stand in uncomfortable and painful silence for a long time. Gray stares at nothing on the frame of the door as a single tear falls from his cheek to his coat.

"What happened?" I finally ask.

"I don't know," he replies despondently. "She's just gone...just gone."

"What about the baby?"

"The boy is fine," he answers.

Rice and I take Gray back home, along with the pot of stew I made. The rest of the evening turns out to be the worst night I have ever lived through. After setting the table, I try to feed a family who has no appetite, and they barely pick at the stew. I spend the evening rocking Betsy's newborn in front of the fireplace. Gray names the baby Benjamin, after Betsy and Rice's dad. While holding little Benjamin, I watch the red and yellow flames dance against the black soot on the back of the fireplace, and I feel a horrible ache in my gut. I feel sad for Betsy who had her whole life in front of her, for Rice losing his sister, Martha and the other children losing their mother, Gray losing his wife, and baby Benjamin, who will never know his beautiful mother who sacrificed her life for him. And I feel awful trepidation for myself, wondering if my birthing bed will hold the same deadly fate in a few short months.

* * *

The funeral is one of the saddest and largest I've ever seen. Gray and the children are devastated by sorrow and grief. Gray does not have a large extended family in Mississippi, but Betsy's family, the Carpenters, fill the church to capacity. Betsy was the eldest of ten children, so the first five pews on either side are filled with her parents, siblings, nieces, and nephews. And with Betsy and her mother being founding members of Fellowship Baptist Church, everyone in the community has made a showing to pay their respects. Following the ceremony, we proceed outside to the cemetery to place Betsy in her final resting place.

As we are speaking with Rice's parents outside the church, I notice young Martha walking arm and arm with a young man along the tree line at the back of the cemetery property, and I wonder if perhaps Martha does indeed have a beau — my brother James.

I soon hear that James has been spending more and more time at Gray's house with Martha. I know they've been friends, as I have seen them together once in a while. But James, who has always been the protective type, is now apparently turning that attribute toward Martha in her time of need. He is consoling her the best way he knows how, just by being there. I know my brother has good intentions, and I know Martha is a beautiful young woman, but I hope in my heart this all turns out well. I would hate for Martha to have her heart broken right after losing her mother. And I would hate for my brother to be the cause of that broken heart.

My fears for them diminish as James and

Martha soon become inseparable. And soon, James asks Gray for Martha's hand. Gray is happy that his daughter will be well taken care of and gives his blessing.

They don't look like typical young lovers giggling and flirting. They are more like old souls, connected through a tragedy that cannot be understood by a casual observer. They tell Daddy that they don't want to have a large wedding celebration with lots of friends and family. They only want a modest ceremony with immediate family and no party. They simply want to hold hands and begin a new life together.

Daddy is used to throwing galas for his children's weddings and is sorely disappointed, but he honors their wishes. He instead gives them the most expensive and extravagant gift he can think of. He gives them Bill, a young strapping, hard-working slave.

Over the next few months, Bill and James build a beautiful and sturdy home on the hundred and sixty acres James purchased on the outskirts of the community. The home is constructed of logs, and has a massive sandstone fireplace in the living room that will be used for cooking as well as for heat. The sandstone comes from Daddy's land. As the rocks are plowed up, they are transported in a wagon to James's house, and he is turning them into a masterpiece of a fireplace.

There is a main room with a high ceiling for the heat to rise. There is also a loft to sleep in, just like Daddy's house. There are a couple windows in the loft with shutters attached. And under the staircase, James leaves room for a pantry to store crocks of preserves and cornmeal and such. Behind the main room are two smaller bedrooms for James and Martha's future children. Behind those is a very large covered back porch.

They are already tilling the land for a garden, and James builds a sturdy chicken coop and a pen for hogs. Their property is coming along nicely and, with Bill's help, quickly. Slowly, the smile is returning to Martha's face.

James has always been the brother who looked out for me. Now, he shows that love and over-protectiveness to Martha. I know in my heart James will make a great father someday, and I can't wait for them to start filling their new house with lots of children.

I don't have to wait long. By the time they move into their new home, it is harvest season, and Martha announces she is pregnant.

I am elated for them.

Children

December arrives, and the weather is cooler. It isn't cold enough to snow — Lord knows it seldom snows here — but the lower temperatures have been creating a coating of frost in the front yard in the mornings. Every day by noon, it is all melted away, and every night, it returns. The harvest is over and the Christmas season is just about to begin. Yesterday morning, Rice walked out to the back of our property and cut down the prettiest pine tree for us to use as our Christmas tree. He loaded it onto a makeshift sled and dragged it back to the house. We placed it in the main room of our house and decorated it with fruit, pine cones, and candles. We hung boughs of pine and holly around the fireplace and over the front door. And the smell of the pumpkin tarts I made yesterday is still lingering in the house today.

Today is December 10th. Today, I give birth to our child. Surprisingly, I do not die in the birthing bed. Remarkably, it is not as terrible as I suspected it might be. The child is a gorgeous little girl, and we name her Martha Lettie Carpenter. I feel well and healthy. As a matter of fact, I feel better than I have in nine uncomfortable months, but my mother and Susannah tell me to stay in bed for a few days and recover. I don't want to lie in a bed when there is the

Christmas holiday to prepare for, but I do as I am told. After two days, I am filled with such boredom from lying around and such excitement for the holiday and the new baby that I can't stay in bed any longer.

Within a few days, we start calling Martha Lettie by the nickname of Mattie. We know there will be too much confusion calling her Martha, due to my having a sister, a sister-in-law, and a niece all named Martha. Our Mattie is a beautiful little blue-eyed girl who shows as much intelligence in her eyes as I saw in Susannah's first child, James Monroe, six years ago. I have never seen my husband beam with such delight and happiness. It is obvious that he is madly in love with his new daughter. I have to laugh when he makes silly faces at her to make her giggle. He hums songs to her, and he rocks her and holds her constantly. In my experience, men are usually a little more hands-off when it comes to raising children, but not Rice. He can't get enough of that baby girl.

As Rice and I cuddle in front of the fireplace, holding our Mattie, he says, "I am the happiest man in the whole state of Mississippi." He leans over and kisses me tenderly.

* * *

I am so excited when James and Martha have their first child—a son—and name him Allen John after our brothers, Allen and John. Right after that, my brother Allen sends word that his wife has delivered their third child, named James Hays. With everyone naming their children after parents and siblings, it is getting more and more difficult to tell who's who when relating a story to someone. I guess that's why we keep coming up with so many nicknames.

Following Allen John's christening, we gather at Daddy's house for a celebration, where my little brother, Hays Jr., announces his upcoming marriage to Loucinda Graham. Loucinda's family is from Pickens County, Alabama, and she is a very strict and proper woman. She is from a well-to-do family and is schooled and well-spoken. There could not be a more suitable match for Hays Jr. and his outspoken personality. He is very religious, very political, and very opinionated. No matter what he says in public, Loucinda agrees with him like his word is Scripture, but I'm sure in private, they have many heated debates, because she is just as opinionated about current events as he is. I get the impression they could start their own country, with Hays Jr. being the supreme leader and Loucinda running everything from behind the scenes.

Their wedding is filled with pageantry and seems almost majestic. He wears a perfect-fitting waistcoat with tails, and she wears an expensive yet modest dress made of wool and trimmed with satin.

Her family arrives in droves from Alabama. All of his political buddies and their fancy wives also make an appearance. Daddy throws quite a party for them at the church, and gives them a large plot of land down the road from his farm as a wedding gift. I suspect Daddy thinks if he doesn't do something drastic, Hays and Loucinda might move to Alabama.

At the wedding, our younger sister, Elizabeth, is introduced to Loucinda's little brother, George Graham, and does not leave his side all evening. Rice and I watch Elizabeth and George from across the room, and we witness young love blossom right before our eyes.

"Remember when we first fell in love like that?" I ask Rice.

He looks at Elizabeth and George and then back at me. "I don't remember falling in love with you. I have loved you since the day I was born," he says.

"Well, remember our first kiss? You used to look at me in a way that I knew you wanted to kiss me. It always gave me butterflies."

Rice reaches up, touches my chin, and turns my face to his. I look into his eyes. I am so mesmerized by them and his touch, I can't speak.

After a few moments of electricity between us, he says, "I know this is your brother's wedding, and I know you'd like to sit here and watch Elizabeth and George all evening, but I have other plans for our evening." He flashes that Carpenter smile and rises to his feet.

I reluctantly pull away from his gaze and look around, hoping no one is witnessing our display of inappropriateness. But I have to admit, I don't think I could stand up right now if I tried. My knees are too weak.

He reaches down, takes my hand, and gently pulls me to my feet. "Mrs. Carpenter, I think we should bid your family a good evening and go home, where I will remind you how much I love you."

We make our rounds, say goodbye to everyone, and head home, hand in hand.

Right after Hays and Loucinda's wedding, I find myself pregnant for the second time. This time I deliver the cutest little boy, who we name Benjamin Hays Carpenter, after Rice's dad and my dad. I thought Mattie was the light of Rice's life until I watch him holding Benjamin for the first time. He beams with happiness, and I realize I have never fully understood the relationship between a father and son until now. Pride is almost radiating from him. He finally has a son. He couldn't be happier. I couldn't be happier.

The delight over the birth of our second child is soon overshadowed by other news. Right after Benjamin is born, my sister Susannah calls a family meeting and announces that her family is moving to Louisiana. Louisiana? I don't even know how far away that is but I suspect the worst. I don't know what I will do without my oldest sister and best friend by my side to share in life's joys and sorrows. When Susannah and her family are packed and ready to leave, we hug and cry and promise to write each other often.

It's almost a year later when I finally receive the first letter.

My dearest sister Mary,

I am writing to you with the happiest of news. I now have seven children, for I have been blessed with a daughter. We have named her Martha Bernice, but I suspect we shall call her Molly, for that is what we have been calling her so far. We are settled into our new home and everyone is happy and healthy. There was a man here in town with some fancy box that puts your image on paper. He calls it a cam-ra or something or other. I wish I could get all of the children to sit still for him, so I could send it to you and you could see how much the children have grown, and of course, see how cute little Molly is. She is so tiny I fear she may break, though I know that could not really happen.

How is Rice? How are the children? I am so sorry it has taken this long to write to you. Between the house, the children, and the pregnancy, I've been just too busy to sit down for five minutes. Please write as soon as you can and tell me all the news. And please tell everyone hello, especially Momma and Daddy.

I love you and miss you.
Your sister,
Susannah Chatham

I am so elated at the thought of another niece. I write Susannah back immediately, telling her how happy I am for her, and I include a tiny pink ribbon for Molly's hair. Toward the end of the letter, I tell her I am happily expecting another child myself.

I can't believe Susannah just had her seventh child. She was married at eighteen and is now thirty-one, so she has birthed a child nearly every other year for the last thirteen years. I'm very happy how my children have been spaced out. I was also married at eighteen, but my children were born when I was twenty and twenty-four, and this child will be born when I am twenty-six. Yes, this is the way it should be. Not seven children that close together. That's just too much work.

In the summer of '54, my son William Travis is born. I name him after my poor deceased brother, William. Mattie and Benjamin have their father's sandy blonde hair and fair skin, but William Travis looks like my side of the family. He has dark brown, almost black hair, and darker skin than the fair Carpenters.

Mattie, who is now seven years old, is such a big help with her little brothers. She loves playing with Benjamin and can't get enough of baby William Travis. We are happy and blessed. The children are a joy. Rice and I are still madly in love, like newlyweds. I feel nothing but bliss every single day. Our lives are perfect. Our farm is doing well and the cotton gin is making money. Our days are filled with farming, housework, raising children, and we love every moment of it.

Mattie attends school daily, and Rice and I spend many evenings after supper watching her write, and listening to her tell us stories about something she learned at school. She is always excited to go to school, and never has any trouble getting out of bed in the mornings.

Benjamin is turning four soon and is anxious to start school next year. He is already trying to copy everything his sister is writing, but he doesn't know what any of it means. The best evenings are when we can hear Mattie and Benjamin in the other room playing school. Mattie is the teacher, and Benjamin is the pupil. She teaches him ABCs and math. They are so funny.

Most days when Mattie goes to school, Benjamin stays at home with me, but on some days, he goes out with Rice and helps him tend crops or just rides on the pony alongside his daddy. I think instead of helping, he is generally in the way, but Rice loves spending the day with him.

Every day, baby William Travis keeps me busy. He is the busiest little bee ever, just into everything. He is much more energetic than either of the other children were, and he starts walking at an earlier age than both of them, too. He is already trying to talk at the age of one and a half, and is the most curious child I have ever seen. If something can be taken apart, William Travis has it undone within moments of getting his hands on it. And he puts everything in his mouth. I am constantly telling him to "spit that out."

This evening, I fall asleep, curled up next to Rice in our comfortable bed, and have a dream that something is dreadfully wrong. I can hear Rice calling my name, but I can't get to him. In my dream, I can't figure out what is happening. I hear Rice calling my name again.

"Mary! Wake up!" Rice yells.

I open my eyes and look around the dark room. I don't know if I'm dreaming or awake.

"Mary! Travis is sick."

"What?" I ask, groggy and disoriented. I think I must still be dreaming, but as I see Rice lighting a candle, I realize something is horribly wrong.

"Mary! Travis is sick. Get up!"

I jump out of bed like a lightning bolt, run toward Travis's little bed, almost knocking Rice out of the way.

"What's wrong with him?" I ask as I remove Travis's blanket.

"I don't know. His cough is awful, and it sounds like he's having trouble breathing," Rice replies, alarm in his voice.

I gently pick him up. He is burning up with fever. I have taken care of sick little ones, from my siblings to Mattie and Benjamin when they were younger, but never in my life have I felt a child this hot. I push down the panic as I hold Travis in my arms and decide what I should do. I know that rocking will soothe him. I know I have to get his fever down. I know he needs more than that.

"Rice," I say calmly, "go get the doctor."

He has already put on his trousers and is heading toward the door. "I'll be back as soon as I can," he says and is gone.

I put Travis back in his bed and run into the kitchen to get the water jug and a cloth. I return to his cradle, take his clothes off, and start washing his body down with the cloth to cool him off. When the cool water touches him, he starts to cry. The crying brings on a coughing fit. His coughing fits are so severe, he can't catch his breath between the coughs. When the coughing stops, he is all but unconscious. When another coughing fit starts, I feel absolute terror, hoping he will be able to catch his next breath, and I find it hard to breathe myself. I feel tears running down my cheeks as I hold him and pray for a miracle the whole time he is coughing. When he finishes coughing, I panic even more, afraid he is not breathing. I watch him like a hawk as his chest goes up and down. His breathing has a rattle to it that I wish I knew how to make go away. It sounds like something is in his lungs. Every time he and I start to relax a little, the coughing starts again. It is a nightmare replaying itself over and over again.

By the time Rice returns with the doctor, Travis is even worse. I try to put some water in him by putting the wet rag in his mouth, but he won't even move his lips or tongue to taste it. I am afraid if he doesn't swallow it and it gets down into his lungs, it might make him worse.

The poor doctor, who has been dragged out of bed in the middle of the night, examines Travis and slowly shakes his head. He says there isn't much he can do. He tells me to keep the boy wet to cool the fever and keep putting drops of water in his mouth to hydrate him. He says there is nothing at all he can do for the cough. All night, I try to soothe Travis by holding him and rocking him, and I pray fervently that he gets better. When the sun rises, I tearfully stay by his cradle. I say prayer after prayer, begging and pleading with God for his recovery. I am frightened. No, I am terrified. The nightmare drags on the entire day, and when the sun sets, I hold Travis in my arms as he takes his last breath.

I hold him for a long time. I don't want to put him down. I sit on the edge of the bed with tears running down my face, holding my dead son for what seems like hours. Finally, I can't take it anymore. I softly kiss the top of his little head and gently place his limp little body back into his crib.

I cover Travis with his blanket, turn to Rice, and say, "Will you please make sure Mattie and Benjamin are in bed?"

I walk out of the room and out the back door of the house. I go out to the barn by myself and cry so long and so hard that I can't even breathe. The grief comes in waves and I deal with it by punching a bale of hay. I'm probably going to break my fingers if I punch any harder, but I don't care.

The pain in my chest is unbearable. I can't control the waves of agony washing over me. I can't stop the waves from coming. I think back to the day we lost Stephen and William and wonder how Momma survived losing two sons on the same day. All death is sad. The deaths of my brothers were tragic beyond words. The death of my son is a million times worse.

When dawn comes and the first ribbons of morning begin to lighten the sky, the rooster crows. I realize I have to get through today and don't really know how I'm going to do it. I compose myself as best I can and go back into the house to make breakfast for Rice and the children. When I enter the kitchen, I see Rice sitting at the table in the dim room. I assume he sat there all night.

I pull out the tub of flour and set it on the table to start making some biscuits.

Rice doesn't move. I light a candle and place it on the table between us.

"I'm so sorry, Mary," he whispers.

"Me, too," I whisper back.

Changes

Early in the morning, a few weeks after we bury William Travis, Daddy comes by the house and asks Rice and me to go for a ride with him. We drop Martha off at school and keep Benjamin with us. I ask Daddy where we are going, but he just says he wants to show us something. Obviously, he is not going to give away his surprise and we will just have to wait. We ride in the crisp morning air for a long, long time before Daddy pulls off the road and stops the wagon in the middle of a field.

"Look," he says, pointing to the right.

"What is that?" Rice asks, rising to his feet in the wagon to get a better look.

"It's our new house," Daddy smiles. "The government granted me some land for my military service back in 1815, so I'm building your mother a new house. But that's not the surprise. Go over and look at it."

On the ground, surrounding the completed foundation, are stacks and stacks of planks. Every house I have ever seen was built of logs, but Daddy has planks. Long, smooth, and all the same size. They are about one inch thick and six inches wide, with tongue and groove edges.

Daddy tells us he had them delivered from the sawmill in the next town, and they are the best lumber money can buy. I am amazed, as usual, at how resourceful Daddy is, and I know it is going to be a beautiful home. This will be the only house in our community built out of planks. He spent the last thirty years working day and night on his farm and raising his children. He is in his mid-sixties now and deserves something this nice to relax in and enjoy in his old age.

Rice actually looks a little green with envy. I poke him in the ribs to make him smile and get the look of jealousy off his face.

As summer begins to give way to the coolness of fall, construction on the house is almost done. It is a dog-trot-style house, with a front and back door and a hallway that connects the two. There is usually one room — or maybe two — on either side of the hallway, but Daddy has put three rooms on either side, which is unheard of. There is usually only one fireplace in a house, but Daddy has two, one placed in each large room on either side of the hallway. The ceiling is twelve feet high with beautiful cross-beams. There are four windows and a covered veranda that runs the entire length of the front of the house. I can't wait to sit out on that beautiful front porch with Momma. There is also a smaller covered veranda in the back of the house. It is simply beautiful. Compared to all the houses I have ever lived in or seen, this is a palace.

My brother, Timothy, went down to Louisiana to stay with Susannah for a while, so the only children Daddy still has at home are the four youngest: Wilson, John, Elizabeth, and Martha Jane. Hays Jr. and Loucinda built a house up the road, and

Elizabeth spends most of her time there with George, who conveniently decided to stay in town following the wedding. From the moment Elizabeth and George met, they have been inseparable. We all know they will get married someday.

Just as Daddy is getting ready for the family to move into the plank house, Elizabeth and George announce they are to be married in a few months. They plan on moving to Pickens County, Alabama, to be closer to George's family. So, even though Daddy is gaining daughters-in-law, sons-in-law, and grandchildren, his core family is getting smaller and smaller. At one time, he had fourteen children. Now, he only has four at home, soon to be three.

I think he makes up for the lack of children by buying slaves. He has about ten slave men who work on the farm and three slave women who take care of the men. He just loves the hustle and bustle of a big family on the farm.

At some point during Daddy's house construction in 1857, Rice asks me to sit down and have a talk.

"I've made a decision," he tells me.

I have no idea what kind of decision he has made and didn't even know that he was contemplating a decision, so I just remain silent and let him continue.

"I've decided that I need to do better for my family and farming is not really the occupation for me. You know I was previously a clerk at a store in town."

I nod. Of course I know. I've known him almost his whole life. But I still don't really understand where this conversation is going.

"Well," he continues, "I've decided to go back into the merchant business. I'm going to sell the farm and we are going to move closer to the center of town and open a general store. I've found a location to build and I've already found a buyer for our house and land."

I didn't realize one could just pack up and change occupations, but that's exactly what we are about to do. It's a little frightening, but also very exciting. Every day, Rice rides into Marion Station and works on the general store, right next to the Mobile & Ohio Railroad track that was built back in 1850. I guess it will be convenient to live next to the railroad track, but I'm not sure. If nothing else, this is a thrilling adventure.

Once the store is built, we fill it with shelves of crackers, hard candy, syrup, cigars, and tobacco. Rice builds a glass display case that holds cloth, pins and needles, ribbons and buttons, and suspenders. We place barrels of coffee beans, oatmeal, spices, and sugar in the center of the store. There are wooden boxes filled with fruits and vegetables. We also order a supply of clothing and hats. We order shoes from Mr. Calhoun, who has made a great success of his leather tannery business here in Marion Station. We order rifles, lanterns, rope, kitchen utensils, pots and pans, and dishes. We are ready to open.

The store is instantly a great success. Rice seems to have a knack for knowing what our customers want before they ask for it. Seldom do we have to tell someone that we do not carry whatever his or her particular need is. Rice seems better at being a merchant than a farmer, and he is much, much happier, which makes me happier.

Above the store, Rice has built a second floor with a main room and two bedrooms that we now call home. This is where I give birth in April of '58 to our fourth child, Charles Clinton. Charlie is a happy, healthy boy, with an infectious smile just like his daddy's. The customers who come into the store smile every time they see him. They seem to look forward to playing with him on their visits, and often say hello to him before they even notice me, which I find humorous.

While Mattie and Benjamin are at school, I carry Charlie around on my hip. When the children come home, Mattie watches her baby brother while I make supper for the family. I have to admit it is easier making supper and taking care of a family when anything I might need is right downstairs.

Living above the store is not only convenient, but we get more news from outside our community and more information about the problems plaguing our country than we ever got before. Our store seems to be the place for men and women to meet and gossip, and it seems that every time the men get together, the conversation inevitably turns to our state's individual rights and the meddling Northern politicians. Lately there has been a new name thrown into the mix—Abraham Lincoln.

Mr. Lincoln is running for president of the United States, and even though it is reported that he said he will not intrude on states' individual rights, many in the South distrust him. In the recent past, taxes have been raised on the goods that Southerners import, making it more and more difficult to do any kind of business and make any kind of profit. It seems like the North is trying to run the entire South out of business and ruin our economy.

The North has now begun putting higher tariffs on our exports. The cotton we are selling overseas is being taxed like there is no tomorrow, as if the North has anything at all to do with our cotton. The bottom line is that we are getting less at auction for our cotton because of the meddling Northerners.

I heard one of the men say that the South is actually paying eighty percent of the country's taxes. I don't know if that is just the men ranting or if it really is true, but either way, our men are becoming more and more upset with the way things are being handled by the Northerners.

I also read in the newspaper recently that there are folks in the North fighting to abolish slavery. I've never thought about slavery one way or another. I never owned a slave, but I do see that some of the people around me, family included, couldn't survive without the work the slaves do. They plant and harvest, build homes and barns, raise children, and many of them, like my dear Bertie, are almost family. I know there are instances when slave children and parents are split up, which breaks my heart. I don't have to imagine the feeling. I know how it feels for a mother to lose a child.

When I was about twenty years old and my little Mattie was almost two years old, I accompanied Daddy to a slave auction at old Mr. Hatcher's place. Mr. Hatcher and his wife had both died of some kind of illness, and the court ordered that all of their belongings be sold and the money used to pay debts and take care of their orphaned children. Not only did they auction off household belongings and farming equipment, but they also auctioned off the slaves.

Mr. Hatcher had a trusted and faithful slave named Cato. Cato was about forty years old. He was strong and in good health, and he sold at the auction for one thousand and fifteen dollars. I thought it was very strange. I had never seen anyone bought or sold like a cow or a hog. And from what I understood, this was not the first time Cato had been sold. However, I imagined this time was different. Cato cared about Mr. Hatcher and this land, and I'm sure he was sad to leave it after Mr. Hatcher's death.

Cato had a wife, Lidey, and Mr. Hatcher had made sure to keep them together. Daddy said since Lidey was blind, she probably wouldn't be worth much at the auction. I didn't know how a blind person would get along in a new place, especially alone, so I was hopeful that Cato and Lidey would be sold together. What I didn't know was that Cato and Lidey also had two children—an infant and a little girl about Mattie's age.

Lidey and her infant were sold for seventy-five dollars for the pair. The almost-two-year-old girl was sold to someone else for two hundred and seventy-five dollars. The man who bought Lidey said he felt bad breaking them up, but he just couldn't afford the little girl, too.

After Lidey and his children were sold to different plantation owners, Cato's face was stoic, but his eyes looked as if his insides were crumbling. I don't know if anyone else at the auction looked at Cato's eyes except me.

I cried all the way home and continued crying for weeks following the auction. I felt so bad for Cato and his family. Imagine a man losing his wife and child, a mother losing her husband and daughter, and a child losing her parents. Selling hogs and horses just isn't the same as selling people. That was my first and last slave auction.

I also know there were instances when slaves were treated very poorly. Probably more instances than I'd ever care to know about. Through some gossiping neighbors, I heard that one of the neighbors' slave girls got upset about something the missus did to her, so the girl tried to poison her with wild jemison weed. An older slave woman saw the girl mash up the weed and add it to the missus's tea. The older woman stepped in and told the girl she would take up the tea, and she sent the young girl outside to do something else. The older woman poured out the tea and made a fresh cup. When the missus's husband came home, the older woman told him what she had seen. I can't say the girl didn't deserve it, but the man was so furious, he tied the girl up to a porch post and whipped her with his horsewhip until she was almost dead.

The only reason we heard the story was because the man's young children saw what was happening and it nearly scared them to death. They ran down the road to get help because they thought their daddy was going to kill the slave girl. The story passed from neighbor to neighbor until I heard it. I never did find out who the slave girl was.

It is bad enough that the North only counts the slaves as three fifths of a person in the Federal census, taking away much of our power in congress, but now there are rumors that some Northern states are really pushing hard to take away the slaves completely. That won't take away much of our work force or our incomes, because most people I know don't even own a slave, but it definitely encroaches on our rights as a free state. And the large property owners, like my daddy, need those slaves to run their plantations.

The tax and slave issues are growing bigger and bigger and seem to be the only things on everyone's minds and lips. Our men are complaining that we are essentially being taxed by the North without having adequate representation in the government, and it looks like it will probably get worse if we don't do something about it. What began in the South as anger has become a fighting spirit and an eagerness to show the North who they are dealing with. We simply will not take this oppression lying down.

* * *

On January 9, 1861, the newspaper headline reads, "Mississippi Secedes from the Union."

We aren't the first state to do so, and from what it says in the newspaper, we won't be the last. The men say that seceding is necessary to protect our state's rights, but they also mumble that things might get worse before they get better, because the North now considers our secession a rebellious act and perhaps even treason.

There are rumors that the North is warning us we cannot secede. We already have, so I don't know what they think they can do about it. They are threatening that they will come down here and force us back into the Union. They call it "reclaiming Federal property." I don't understand how they think our land is Federal property, or how they think reclaiming it will be possible, but every man I know is talking about fighting the North and going to war.

A sunny spring morning, a local politician rides into town and starts a political rally right outside our store. He is trying to get our men to join forces to fight the North. After a small crowd gathers, he stands on our front porch and starts his speech.

"It is the honorable obligation of every man here to defend his home and our new country, the Confederate States of America."

He pauses for applause and receives a rousing ovation. When the cheer diminishes, he continues, "The wickedness that is taking over the North must be stopped. We will not accept the label of rebels, we will not accept the label of traitors, and we will certainly not accept their definition of treason, as we are justly protecting our rights as a free state. Rise up with me, my countrymen, and let us be swift and just in the eyes of God. Our glory will not be diminished. Our freedom will not be overthrown. We will rise up for our rights, for our families, for our freedom, for our land, and for our country."

The small crowd cheers with an excitement that I have never before seen. I really don't like all this talk of war, but I have to admit, the man is very impressive, and by the time he finishes his speech, I swear I am ready to saddle up my horse and ride myself.

All through the spring of '61, men are having meetings and rallies and signing up to fight the North if the occasion eventually arises.

In June, I receive a letter from my sister Susannah down in Louisiana. She writes that my dear nephew, James Monroe Chatham, who is now a young man of nineteen, has signed up to fight the North and has already left for training. She writes that he is going to train at a place called Camp Moore. I am so proud of that boy and the man he is becoming. I always knew he would do something great with his life. I feel I may burst with pride.

Everyone around me is riled up and ready to go to war. I try to ignore the negativity and the war talk as I find myself again with child right after the harvest. I feel great trepidation and uneasiness about bringing a child into this mess, yet at the same time, I am so very excited to hold another baby. With my children growing older — Mattie is now thirteen, Benjamin is ten, and Charlie is three — I so long for another tiny baby to hold. Rice is such a good father, and I know he will be overjoyed to have another infant in the house.

As I am biding my time, waiting for the right moment to tell him, I receive another letter from Susannah. I open it in the store, anticipating happy news of her latest adventures. I also hope there will be word of my nephew, the brave soldier.

My dear sister,

It is with great sadness that I write this letter. It is about your nephew, James Monroe Chatham. Only a few days ago, we learned of his death at Camp Moore. He went there to train in May. We have only received one letter from him since that time, stating that he was well and working hard. We haven't gotten many details of his death as of yet, but it seems he died of illness. The letter I received said there was an epidemic of measles at the camp and he died October 28th. I will write again when I can.

With love,
Your sister,
Susannah Chatham

My heart stops beating. This can't possibly be my beautiful James Monroe. It must be someone else with the same name. They must have two young men by that name at Camp Moore. I read the letter again. As the truth sinks in, my knees collapse. I fall down to the floor, clenching the paper in my hand. I have to go tell Momma and Daddy. How in the world will I tell them?

Benjamin enters the room at that moment. Surprised to see me on the floor, he asks if something is wrong.

"Where is your father?" I ask him.

"He's down at Mr. Calhoun's place, buying new boots for the store."

"Benjamin, you and I have to go to see Grandma and Grandpa. Hurry, boy, saddle up the horse and let's go," I order.

As Benjamin runs out the door to do as he is asked, I shakily rise from the floor and smooth down my dress, brushing the dirt off the bottom. I yell up the stairs to Mattie to come down and mind the store for a little while. I gently fold the letter and tuck it away in my pocket. I don't want Mattie to see her cousin's name on the letter while I am gone. I put on my bonnet and take a few deep breaths. Mattie comes down the stairs carrying little Charlie in her arms. I tell her that Benjamin and I have to go to Grandma and Grandpa's house, and we will return soon.

"If your father comes home before we do, tell him we will be back shortly."

Benjamin appears in the doorway a few minutes later and says the horse is saddled and ready to go. He and I ride as fast as we can toward Daddy's house.

Upon being told the news, Momma collapses in her big chair, and Daddy stares silently at the floor. Without a word, he hastily walks out the back door, letting it slam. The noise makes me jump. I decide to follow him.

"Daddy, are you all right?"

"No!" he says sharply, then he turns to me and adds, "You know I've lost children before, but James Monroe is my first grandchild. James Monroe just can't be dead. It just ain't right."

He steps off the porch and walks toward the field without looking back. When Daddy is upset, he works. When Daddy is angry, he works. When Daddy is anything, he works. That is his way of dealing with things, and I know I can't say anything to ease his pain, so I stand there and helplessly watch him walk away.

I return to the dim living room and sit with Momma for a little while, both of us trying to comprehend that James Monroe is really gone. We question Susannah's state of mind, but we know we can do nothing for her. We hold hands and say a prayer for God to watch over Susannah and her remaining family, and we leave it in God's hands. I then rise from my chair and tell Momma that I need to get Benjamin back home before dark. I walk out the front door and leave Momma alone, sitting in her big chair in front of the empty fireplace.

Through my heartache for my sister, Susannah, and the awful feeling in my gut over the loss of my precious James Monroe, I somehow waddle my way through another pregnancy. The spring finally makes its way through the dark clouds of winter. The birth of my darling new son brings the sun back into my life. I name him Monroe Franklin Carpenter.

I write Susannah a letter, telling her I have named my newborn after her son. Susannah sends word back that she is very pleased and sends her blessings to little Monroe Franklin.

Quick Marriages

After months of hearing that the North is going to invade the South and force the seceded states back into the Union, the rumors seem to be coming true. Men are organizing forces all over the country, and our little community in Mississippi is no exception. Lauderdale County organizes the 41st Infantry Regiment, the Cole Guards. My four younger brothers—Timothy, Hays Jr., Wilson, and John—immediately sign up at Marion Station, though Wilson tells the boys he is going to stay behind and help Daddy plant and will catch up with the company as soon as he is finished. My dear husband and his brother Hilliard are also among the first men to volunteer.

We are all so proud of our men, yet we wonder how long they will be gone, and how we will take care of the farms and stores while they are away.

"Mary, we won't be gone very long. This won't take long at all," Rice assures me as we sit at the table eating breakfast.

"How long is 'not long,' Rice?"

"It will probably only take a couple weeks, maybe a few months at the most."

I pout as I get up from my seat and walk around the table. "I hope you're right. I'm going to miss you," I say as I sit on his lap and wrap my arms around his neck.

"You know these Yankees are soft," he says as he puts his arms around my waist. "We'll whip them before breakfast and be home before the harvest." He smiles that Carpenter smile and I know he is right.

It will be fast and he will be home before I know it. I bend my head and kiss him.

"I'll miss you every minute," I whisper.

"I'll miss you, too, Mrs. Carpenter." He kisses me again.

Our boys are so full of bravado, how can they lose? The North can't just come into our homes and lives and start telling us what to do and how to live. Our country was built on individual freedom. Our state's freedoms cannot simply be taken away by other states. We'll show those Yankees who is in charge around here, and they won't know what hit them.

Before the men leave, the fancy women throw cotillions and parties to raise money for supplies. All the women sew uniforms for their brave men, and the men will be smartly dressed in gray suits with yellow cummerbunds.

After all of the war talk and all those long months of preparation, I can't believe the day has finally arrived for Rice and my brothers to move out.

On an early May morning, at Marion Station, right in front of our store, the men gather and are ready to leave. Everyone within fifty miles comes to wish them well and send them off in style. The street is boldly decorated with banners and flags. Our new

Confederate States of America flag, the Stars and Bars, is flying over every business and every house, and people are waving smaller versions sewn onto sticks. The first Stars and Bars only had seven stars for the seven states that seceded, but our flag now has thirteen stars. Hopefully, we will be able to put more stars on it. There is a band playing "Dixie" between rousing speeches about honor and freedom and victory. There are barbecues and picnics and parades and flag-waving, and everyone is jubilant and full of pride for our young men. We are all fully and confidently expecting them to return home before harvest. I stand on the front porch of our store, smiling and waving my flag like I am the proudest woman in Mississippi, but inside, I am frightened by the prospect of what could happen. My heart is aching at the thought of not having Rice around for who knows how long. He assures me yet again that the war will end quickly, probably before they even get to the front and load their guns. He also tells me we have no choice. We have to do what is right. We have to keep our freedom. I know he is right, but I'm still sick to my stomach with worry. I smile and kiss him and hug him and I don't want to let go.

Our tearful goodbyes mix with rousing cheers. The men proudly march down the road to the sound of the band playing. I try not to think of my nephew dying for this cause. I try to remind myself that he could have died of the measles anytime and anywhere. I try to ignore the feeling of my heart crumbling and the paralyzing fear that I may never see my brothers or my beloved Rice again. I can't allow myself to think like that. I smile, I wave my flag, and I stand tall, but behind my smile, I can't breathe.

Daddy and Momma stand on the porch of the store with me, waving their flags, too. Momma looks like she is feeling the same way I am. She has four sons going off to war; she has to be frightened. Daddy looks a little jealous that he is too old to join the boys on their great adventure.

After we send the boys off and the crowd disperses, Daddy and Momma kiss me goodbye and remind me that this war won't take long. They head home in their wagon, waving as they disappear down the road.

* * *

Included in the muster of boys who are going to fight are our town's most eligible young bachelors, and there are just as many young girls who want to be a part of the excitement. What young girl would not want to marry a hero? Two of my siblings are included in that excitement.

Wilson stays to help Daddy plant, with the intention of catching up with his brothers when he is finished. This also gives him time to court Miss Sarah Graham. Wilson and Sarah are quickly married by the justice of the peace, and I am happy to see my little brother with such a beautiful girl.

My little sister, Martha Jane, is also wrapped up in the excitement. She promises to marry Martin Warren before he leaves. He has signed up for a different company, the 8th Regiment, Mississippi Infantry, and is also staying behind for the planting. He will head out immediately once it's complete.

Daddy wants to throw Martha Jane a big, lavish wedding, but there is no time for that. Martin is leaving soon, but he promises her he will give her the world when he returns as a hero. Martha Jane is smitten with young, handsome Martin, and flattered by the attention given to her by the other girls who wish to marry a hero also. She gives up her dreams of a big wedding to marry her brave and courageous soldier in a quick ceremony at the local courthouse without Momma or Daddy present.

As the months pass, Wilson's bride, Sarah, finds herself pregnant. She tells me she is worried and upset because she wrote to Wilson but did not hear back from him. I try to assure her that he is probably just busy, or maybe the company has moved and he did not even receive the letter. I tell her I haven't heard from Rice, either. As wives of heroes, we just need to be patient. Sarah stays with her momma and daddy at their house and waits patiently for word from Wilson. We don't see much of her as she more or less keeps to herself.

Newlywed Martha Jane's romantic ideals crumble quickly. The town tries to keep up morale by having picnics, parties, and rallies, but Martha Jane cannot flirt with the boys as she did in the past so she refuses to attend the functions.

This morning at Momma's house, I walk in on Martha Jane sitting at the table, pouting.

"What's wrong, Martha Jane?" I ask.

"What's wrong?" she whines. "I'm not going

to the picnic today! That's what's wrong."

"Why not? It'll be fun to visit with everyone."

She pouts, "It won't be any fun at all. I'll have to sit on the sidelines because I can't talk to any of the boys."

"Martha Jane, there aren't going to be any boys there. They are all off fighting," I assure her, though I know it's useless.

"See? That's just what I mean."

I'm confused, and I'm sure I don't want to know the answer, but I ask anyway, "What? I don't understand."

"That's just what I mean. Not only can I not talk to any boys because I'm a married lady, I can't talk to any boys because they are all off fighting some stupid war. It's just not fair."

I sigh at her, unable to follow her twisted logic. Finally I say, "Martha Jane, it's just a picnic. I don't really understand what you are talking about."

She rolls her eyes and speaks to me like I'm five years old. "What I am saying is that this war is a big ole joke."

"A joke?"

"Yes, a joke, being played on me."

She storms out of the house and lets the back door slam on her way out.

I let her go, not willing to even try to comprehend her train of thought.

Both Sarah and Martha Jane become lonely and disheartened, but while Sarah has a pregnancy and eventually a new baby daughter to keep her occupied, Martha Jane only becomes more bored and resentful. This only shows how spoiled she really is. I ask Martha Jane to come live with me and the children. I explain to her that she can help with baby Monroe and help in the store and socialize and talk to people, instead of sitting in Daddy's house feeling sorry for herself and her self-imposed lack of freedom. She refuses for a long, long time, but eventually she shows up on my doorstep with a basket of clothes and her bonnets in hand.

We only have two bedrooms above the store. The children share one, and baby Monroe and I share the other. I don't know what kind of arrangement Martha Jane thought she was coming into, but the look on her face is not a happy one when I show her to my room and explain that we will share it. I have the sinking feeling Martha Jane is going to be more work than any of my children, but it is too late to send her back now. And I really am looking forward to her company. She may be spoiled, but she is my funny and sweet little sister, and I am so excited to have her around. I am hoping that she will help me pass the time, because my home and my life are utterly empty and void without Rice.

War 1862

In June, I receive a letter from my brother Timothy. He writes that he is sick, though not gravely, and is in a Confederate hospital. He says when he feels better, he will immediately go back to camp with his brothers, although he would love to come home and see Momma and Daddy and his nieces and nephews. Timothy has always been a loving boy who is deeply attached to his family. The letter doesn't mention if he is homesick, and maybe he doesn't feel that way because he has been with his brothers, but I'm sure he does not like being far away from home, and he certainly doesn't like being alone in a hospital. Even though he is not quite a huggy-kissy kind of boy, he always looks to be surrounded by other family members. If he goes hunting, he asks someone to go with him. If he sits on the porch, it is only because someone else is already there. If he runs into town for something, he always drags someone along. I can just imagine how lonely he feels in a hospital without any family around him.

In his letter, he asks for prayers and ends the letter with, "Yours for as long as life shall endure, Timothy Rodgers."

All summer, friends in the community receive letters from their husbands, sons, and brothers, and since everyone picks up their mail at the store, they always immediately open them there. We are so proud of our brave men, and everyone loves sharing their excitement over every little piece of news. In the letters, some men complain of the living conditions. Some just say how much they miss everyone at home. Most write of the soaring prices and awful inflation that has begun. All beg for letters and news from home.

As the harvest grows near, I wonder about Rice's promise. He said they would be home by harvest. I hope he is right. I also wish every day that I would receive a letter from him. Every time anyone stops in the store to pick up his or her mail, I feel a little touch of resentment. I miss Rice so much, and I know the children do, too. At least one of them asks me every single day when their daddy is going to return. I don't have an answer so I simply say, "Soon."

In October, six months from the day he left, I finally receive a letter from Rice.

My dearest Mary,

On the 20th of September, all of our training and drills paid off. We had our first major battle at Iuka. Before that, we were in Corinth, and I've heard rumors that we are either heading back to Corinth or on to Kentucky. I will let you know when I arrive at either place.

I'm doing well but was hoping to be home by now. There is not much to eat here and my shoes are wearing thin, but I am excited to come home soon and tell you all the things I have seen. Please write back to me when you get this letter, and let me know how you and the children are doing. And please do the best you can with the store until I come home. It shouldn't be too long. I know there is no chance of getting a furlough to come home and see you right now.

Tell my father that this morning I drank a cup of coffee with a Yankee. He is a prisoner, and I gave him a cup of coffee. I think my father will laugh at that. Tell your father that except for Timothy getting sick, his sons here are well. I don't know if you know that they sent Timothy to the hospital because he was sick, but we expect him to be back with us soon.

Please write to me when you receive this and let me know how you are.

Your loving husband,
Rice Carpenter

I write him back immediately.

My dearest Rice,

I am so happy to hear from you, and I miss you terribly. I worry so about you and am grateful that you are well. I will pass those messages on to our fathers.

Yes, Timothy wrote to me and said he is anxious to get back to camp. The companies have started sending out casualty and wounded lists, and I post them in the store. Many of the community members come here daily to *look at them. So far, I do not know any name on the lists and that is a blessing.*

It is also a blessing that people come here so often to see the lists, because they also buy things when they are here. Your store is doing so well and making a good amount of money. When you come home, you will be very happy.

Your children and I are all well, though we will be more well and good when you come back. I would like this war to end very soon.

Goodbye for now, my love.
Your loving wife,
Mary Carpenter

Benjamin and I ride over to Momma and Daddy's house to tell them we heard from Rice. We stop at my brother and sister-in-law's house along the way to share the news.

My brother James and his wife—Rice's niece Martha—are certainly filling their house with lots of babies. They now have five children. After Allen John, they have two girls, Lizzie and Ellen. The girls are followed by a boy, Willie, and the baby, Pernecia Ann, whom we call Necie.

Necie is four years old now, and if you asked her how old she is, she will hold up four fingers and hold down her thumb with the other hand. Martha keeps her in pigtails, and I could just pinch her cheeks nonstop every time I see her. The children are happy and healthy, and just as I suspected, Martha makes beautiful babies and James is turning out to be a wonderful and overprotective father.

When we pull up at James and Martha's house, their children are all playing in the front yard and on the front porch.

"Where's your momma?" I ask Allen John, who is standing barefoot and dirty on the porch.

"She's inside," he replies. "She says she isn't feeling well and asked me to keep the little ones busy."

"What do you mean she isn't feeling well? Is she sick? You should have come to get me, Allen John."

He shrugs his shoulders and throws a carved wooden ball toward Benjamin.

"I asked her if she wanted me to go get someone, but she told me no."

I tell Benjamin to stay outside and play with his cousins while I hurry inside to check on Martha.

The inside of the house is almost too much to bear. It is stifling hot, humid, and smelly. If you didn't know someone in the house is sick, you would be able to tell by the smell the moment you enter the front door. It is dim and dark, as there are no candles lighting any of the rooms, no oil lamps burning, no food cooking in the fireplace. It looks like no one lives here at all. I walk directly toward the bedroom.

"Martha?" I call as I walk through the parlor. When I enter the bedroom, I see her.

Martha not feeling well is an understatement. She is lying in bed in a puddle of sweat, with her hair matted to her forehead. She is burning up with fever and complaining of a headache and a stomach ache.

She is also coughing in between words.

"Who's there?" she answers and coughs.

"It's Mary Ann. Are you ill?"

She coughs again.

James is lying next to her in the bed, but I can't see him very well in the darkness of the room. He doesn't wake as I speak to Martha. It is difficult to see him, and I don't hear him snoring. I'm beginning to think he is not breathing, but I don't want to startle or frighten Martha by asking.

"How long have you felt like this, Martha?" I ask her as I light the candle on her bedside table and glance over at James.

"I don't know," she hoarsely whispers, "maybe," —cough— "a couple weeks." Cough. "I think I'm getting worse. And my stomach hurts so much, I can't stop going to the outhouse. James got sick first and then I got sick."

I run into the kitchen, soak some cloths, and fill a cup with water. I bring them back to the room and place a wet cloth on Martha's forehead. I walk around to James's side of the bed to put the cloth on his forehead. He is ice cold and indeed he is not breathing. I can't see the color of his skin, but I imagine his lips are blue. He is gone.

I freeze for a moment. I try to stay composed as I push the alarm and terror way, way down inside. I go back around to Martha's side of the bed and try to get her to sip some water, but she is coughing too violently and gives up. She lays her head back on the pillow and closes her eyes.

"I'm going to go get some help," I tell her, trying to hide the panic and nervousness in my voice.

"Will you be all right for a little bit?"

Martha nods and immediately drifts off to sleep. I sit on the edge of the bed and watch her for a few minutes while I decide what to do. I can't tell her James is dead, but I can't leave her lying next to him.

I can't cry right now. I have to do something. I can't ask the children to carry their dead father out of the house. I can't stay here and take care of Martha. I have my own children to get home to, and I'm not going to bring my children back here and take a chance of them getting sick. I can't send my sister, Martha Jane, down here. Lord knows that girl can barely take care of herself, much less an ailing adult, five children, and a dead brother.

I could go ask Momma to send Bertie or to come here herself to take care of Martha. What do I do about James? I stand up, look over at him, and fight back the tears for my sweet over-protective brother.

Wait. I can't send Momma or Bertie here with James lying dead in the bed. I have to do something else and I have to do it right now, but what?

I decide to go get Daddy.

I hurry out the front door and tell Benjamin to watch his little cousins. "Under no circumstances are you or your cousins to go into the house and bother Uncle James and Aunt Martha. Do you understand me, Benjamin?" I say with more authority than I have ever used on any of the children before.

Benjamin relies with a simple, "Yes, ma'am."

Then I tell Allen John to come with me. I want to ask him some questions about his parents' illnesses on the way to get Daddy.

As we ride quickly down the dusty path, Allen John says his mother and father haven't really been themselves for a couple weeks. "Daddy was feeling tired and feverish for a while. Then, last week, Momma got sick and wouldn't get out of bed at all. I yelled in to ask her if they needed anything or if I should go get someone, but she always said no. She just told me to take care of the little ones so they wouldn't come around her and get sick, too. When are they going to start feeling better, Aunt Mary? I'm getting tired of taking care of these children."

"I don't know, Allen John. We'll get your grandma or Bertie to come help, and why don't you children come home with me tonight, all right?"

That seems to put a smile on his face.

When Allen John and I arrive at Momma and Daddy's house, it looks deserted. There is no lamplight in the windows and no smoke coming from the chimney. Daddy is not outside working on some project as he always is. There is no bustling of slaves around the house or in the fields that I can see. I have never seen the place so eerily quiet.

"Momma, are you here?" I call as Allen John and I step up onto the covered front porch.

"Who's there?" Momma yells from inside.

"It's me, Momma. Mary Ann. I have Allen John with me. What's going on around here?" I ask, opening the front door.

"You should probably stay out, Mary. And make Allen John stay out on the porch," she yells back.

I nod to Allen John to stay outside, and I poke my head inside the door to see what in the world is happening. My mother is sitting in her big chair in the front room, fanning herself lethargically. She doesn't even look up when I enter the room.

"I think there's something going around," she says, slumped in her chair with her eyes closed. "Bertie and some of the slaves got sick a week ago, and now I'm not feeling so well myself. Your father is lying down with a headache. When have you ever known that man to lie down in the middle of the day? Bertie is in the back room, asleep. I told all them slaves to go home until tomorrow. I can't deal with them while I'm taking care of Bertie and your father. Something is really wrong with Bertie. She's so sick, she's almost delirious sometimes. She goes between being very agitated and calm. I don't know what is wrong with her. It's not like her to be agitated. If they're not better tomorrow, I'm going to send for the doctor."

I kneel down on the floor at Momma's feet, fold my hands in her lap, and whisper, "Momma, I have some bad news. Martha is sick, too. I need some help over there. I think James is not so good, Momma. I don't want Allen John to hear me say it, but I think..." I hesitate, trying to hold back the tears.

"What is it, Mary?" Momma sits up a little in the chair and looks at me with sudden concern on her face.

"Momma, I think James is dead."

Momma freezes. I put my head in her lap and shed my first tear for James the protector. Why didn't anyone protect him? And who will now protect his wife and children? And me? Who will protect me with Rice off fighting?

Momma sits still and stares at nothing on the wall as she slowly and absentmindedly strokes my hair.

Finally, she speaks as if she has just realized something. "Oh, no."

She pauses and stops rubbing my head for a moment. I look up at her.

"How are we going to tell your father?" she asks. A single tear rolls down her cheek.

"I don't know, Momma."

After a few minutes, I realize I need to look elsewhere for help.

"Listen, Momma, I can see that you and Bertie can't help Martha right now, so I need to go and find someone else. I'm sorry I have to leave, but I need to go get help. Will you tell Daddy I was here, please?" I stand up to leave. I bend over and kiss her on the top of her head. She is still holding my hand and I have to pull it away from her.

"Sure I will, Mary. Your daddy will be disappointed to have missed you. I will tell him about James, and we will come to Martha's as soon as everyone here is feeling better," she says as I walk toward the door.

When I reach it, I turn back to look at her in the dim room, realizing that I didn't even tell her about the letter I received from Rice. I don't think she would really care about it at this point, so I let it go. As I open the door, I look back at her again and think she is just a small shadow in her big chair. She reaches up to wipe a tear from her face, and then sighs all of the air out of her. She looks even smaller. Before I leave, I promise her I will come back in a few days and visit.

I walk out onto the front porch and close the door. Allen John asks, "What's going on in there, Aunt Mary?"

"I think everyone around here has the same thing your momma has. Let's go down the road and see if my sister-in-law Harriet can help us."

Rice is the eighth of ten children. Harriet is his older sister, and his younger sister is Mary Louise. Harriet, her husband William Jolly, and their four children live right down the road from Momma and Daddy. Mary Louise lives on the other side, next door to Harriet and William. When we arrive at Harriet's house, both sisters are in rocking chairs on the front porch, shucking corn.

"Hi, Harriet. Hi, Mary Louise. I'm so glad you're both here," I say while climbing down from the horse.

"My goodness, Mary, hello. What brings you all the way out here?" asks Harriet as she rises from her chair and heads off the porch toward us.

I turn to my nephew and say, "Allen John, will you please go in the house and get a cup so I can get some water from the well? I'm just dying of thirst from this heat."

I fan myself and wait for him to move before continuing my conversation with Harriet and Mary Louise. I try not to cry, but a single tear rolls unchecked down my face and I quickly rub it off with the back of my hand. I look at Harriet and see the concern on her face as she watches me, but she doesn't say anything. She is a very intuitive woman and doesn't miss much. Allen John is an obedient boy. He immediately ties up the horse and nods a greeting to the ladies as he hurries past them on his way into the house.

Harriet yells after him, "Boy, there are some peaches on the back porch. Why don't you get us a few of those? And there's a bucket back there, too. Bring that so your horse can get a drink." She speaks to Allen John, but her eyes are on me, knowing something is wrong.

As soon as Allen John is out of earshot, I blurt everything out. "I need your help. Allen John's mother is very, very sick. I tried to get Momma to come over there with me, but apparently everyone in her house is sick, too. I also have some bad news about my brother, James. He has been sick too, and I think he might be dead. He's lying in the bed...with Martha. He's not breathing. Can one of you fetch the doctor and one of you come with me to help take care of Martha? I will take her little ones home with me tonight, but I can't stay at her house and nurse her all night. I have my own little ones expecting me." I speak as fast as I can, hoping to finish before Allen John comes back into earshot.

Harriet and Mary Louise both start moving at the same time. They don't ask any questions. Harriet says she will get her husband and come right behind me to Martha's house. Mary Louise says she will go fetch the doctor and meet us there.

By the time we all meet back at Martha's house, Martha is worse. The doctor confirms that James is dead and says there isn't much he can do for Martha. Harriet's husband, William, has followed us to the house, and he and the doctor take James's body out of the house while Martha is sleeping and I have the children occupied behind the house, picking the last of the vegetables from the fall garden.

The doctor tells me James has been dead for at least a day. 'Oh, my good Lord,' is the first and only thing that goes through my head. Then it really hits me that my dear James is gone. James always took care of everyone. Now what will Martha do? And what about his poor children? Poor, poor James.

The doctor says Martha seems to have typhoid fever and hopefully will improve by next week. I have heard of typhoid fever, and what the doctor says is true. It will run its course and one will improve next week. Or it will burst your insides and you will be dead next week, like my poor brother James. There is no in between.

They take James's body directly to the cemetery in William's wagon, and with the help of Bill the slave, they dig a grave to bury him. The pastor says prayers over him, and he is buried in a plain wooden coffin in an unmarked grave on the grounds of Fellowship Baptist Church. There is no family funeral.

Harriet and Mary Louise take turns nursing Martha while I watch all of the children.

The following Sunday, Martha is dead.

Foster Parent

I take care of James and Martha's orphans while Rice's sisters, Harriet and Mary Louise, take care of Martha's funeral service arrangements. On a sunny Tuesday morning at 9 a.m., we bury Martha next to James in a plain wooden coffin.

Following the funeral service, we all take turns putting a flower on Martha's grave as we exit the cemetery grounds. I feel like I am melting inside. Martha and James were just too young to be taken from us. James has always been my favorite brother, and he is gone far too soon for no reason. A fever? Four of my brothers are fighting in a war. James stays home and dies of a fever? It's ironic and so painfully sad.

And poor, beautiful Martha, with her sandy blonde hair and her Carpenter smile. She was only thirty years old. I have been so busy with all of the children that I haven't even had time to cry over James or Martha.

I look out across the cemetery at all the headstones and feel a deep ache in my gut. There is nothing I can do to fix it. I wish Rice would come home. I just want him to hold me and let me cry. I want him to wrap his arms around me and take away the pain. I just want to see his face and his beautiful smile, and then have him reassure me that everything will be all right. I am so lost and lonely without him. I close my eyes for a second and will myself not to fall on the ground and cry like a baby.

There is no one around to take in James and Martha's five orphans except me or Loucinda. And she is not blood family. Daddy is still sick. Allen lives far away. Lewis, Susannah, and Elizabeth live in different states. The rest of the boys are off fighting. Once Daddy is feeling better, I will speak with him about the children, but for now, I will have to keep them with me.

I love my nieces and nephews but have no idea how I'm going to feed and clothe them without help. Hopefully, Rice will be home soon. How in the world am I going to take care of my four children and James's five until Rice returns? I look up at the sky and silently plead with God to send Rice home.

The smallest of the orphans, Necie, doesn't seem to really understand what is going on, but Allen John, the oldest, is very sad and sullen. I remember how deeply it hurt to lose two brothers, my son Travis, and again to lose my nephew, James Monroe Chatham, but I can't even fathom how lost these children must be feeling after losing their father and mother. If I lost my parents, I would crumble, and I'm a grown-up. As we walk toward the road, with the red clay under our feet and the smell of the pine trees in the air, I pick up four-year-old Necie, place her on my hip, and hug her to my chest.

She touches my hair with her little fingers, and then touches my cheek and pulls my face around to look at her. She looks me in the eye. With her pigtails bouncing with each step, she says, "I want to go home to Momma now. Where is Momma?"

Tears sting my eyes as I turn away and look down at Allen John, then back at Necie, then straight ahead at the road without answering her. Allen John stares off into the distance with pain in his eyes. I wish Rice would come up behind Allen John and put his hand on the boy's shoulder with that reassuring kindness he always shows. But that is only a dream and it's not going to happen. I need to be the strong one right now, though it is everything I can do to not break down and cry right here in front of the children.

I wrap my arm around Allen John's shoulder and say, "Let's go back to my house and make something to eat."

We walk down the dirt road toward the store in silence in the warm afternoon sun. The children are quiet, James's and mine. The only sound besides the gravel under our feet is the occasional bird or bullfrog.

Necie lays her head on my shoulder and falls asleep. Mattie walks behind us, holding hands with her brothers. Allen John walks by my side and never says a word. Seven-year-old Willie is walking on the other side of me, holding on to my skirt. Lizzie walks ahead of us with a boy she knows, and Ellen is about a mile behind us, walking alone. Poor little things. I wish I could make them feel better.

That afternoon, I put all the vegetables I have in the kitchen into a pot to make stew. As I stir it, I think that it is not enough for all of us to eat. Fortunately, no one is going to have much of an appetite. However, I wonder how long the children will be staying with me, and what we will eat tomorrow and the day after.

I don't have a farm to raise crops or animals to butcher, and the store is getting emptier and emptier. We have a couple chickens for eggs, a hog, and a horse in the field behind the store. That is it.

All of my customers are friends, family, and neighbors. I recently began to allow them to buy most things on credit. For a while, I would trade things they needed for things I needed, like milk and vegetables. But with this war going on so long, there isn't much to trade with these days, and at this point, there is barely enough food for my four children, let alone adding five more mouths to the bunch. Most of the men from the community are off fighting, so most of the farms are at a standstill. A majority of the fall harvest is still in the fields and it is the end of November.

With the rising inflation, our currency is quickly losing its value, so I figure allowing the customers to use credit is not a bad idea, whether our currency bounces back or dwindles altogether. However, without making money, there is no way to buy new supplies for the store.

After we eat our small bowls of stew in painful silence, I help the children wash up and put them all to bed. They are so sad and it breaks my heart. I kiss them all goodnight. After I sit on the bed and brush out little Necie's pigtails, which become the prettiest blonde ringlets, I tuck her in bed for the night.

She looks up at me and again asks, "When will I go home to see Momma?"

Her little voice makes me ache.

I have to be honest with her, and in the gentlest way I can phrase it. "Oh, baby, you always have your momma and your home right here in your heart." I gently pat her chest. "Close your eyes and picture your momma's face."

Necie closes her eyes, and in the candlelight, I can see a smile come to her lips.

"There. Now, you drift off to sleep and dream about your beautiful momma. You're going to stay here with your aunt Mary for a little while. Aunt Mary will be right outside the door, and Aunt Mary loves you very, very much."

I kiss her forehead and blow out the candle. I sit on the edge of the bed and hum a lullaby until she falls asleep. When she starts breathing more deeply, I remain quietly in the dark and think about what Reverend Jones said many years ago at my brothers' funeral. He spoke of sharing our time and our love, even though we never know if that time will be long or painfully short. He said we need to be a witness for each other's lives, because life is worth nothing unless there is someone to notice it.

I think of James and his sweet wife, Martha, and my eyes well up with tears. As the silent tears drip from my face onto my dress, in my heart I make a vow that I will be a witness for James and Martha. I will make sure their children know what special parents they had. I will always remind them how much they were loved by their mother and father. The older I become, the more that hillside funeral makes sense to me. I reluctantly stand up, bend over, kiss Necie on the forehead again, and leave the room.

After I quietly close the bedroom door, I light the oil lamp on the wooden table, gather some paper, a nib pen, and some ink. I sit down and write Rice a letter.

My dearest husband,

I hope this letter finds you well. I miss you more than words can say.I am taking this opportunity to write to you in light of our current events. My heart is so heavy, and I don't know how to tell you any of this gently, so I'm just going to come out with it.

I have buried my brother James and his wife. They both died of the fever in the last couple weeks. The doctor could do nothing for them. I am so sorry. I have brought their children home with me until we figure out what is best for them.

Daddy is not well enough to discuss it right now, for he has been sick, too. There seems to be some kind of fever going around. The doctor said it may be typhoid fever. Bertie had it the last couple weeks, but Momma said she is better now. Bertie is going to come over tomorrow and help with the children for a few days. And my sister, Martha Jane, is here to help also.

Please stay safe and know that I love and miss you. Please write when you can.

I remain your loving wife eternally,
Mary Ann Carpenter

Illness

If the war isn't already the worst thing anyone has ever endured, it seems that every single person around me is sick. When Bertie came over yesterday to help with the children, she said that Daddy is not doing well at all. As a matter of fact, he is worse. This typhoid fever—if that's what it is—is the worst illness I have ever witnessed. It starts with a mild fever, headache, and maybe a cough. It progresses to a higher fever and some kind of delusion. Some sick people are picking invisible things out of the air, or picking at the same spot on a quilt for hours at a time. Some just sleep through the high fever. The third week of the illness is the worst. It comes with severe stomach pains and many, many trips to the outhouse. This is the week that is the most frightening. The ailing person either gets better within a few days, or dies from his or her insides rupturing. The doctor says there is nothing he can do for these people. There is no medicine to treat this fever.

Just about everyone in town is sick at the same time. It seems like every single household has at least one person who is fighting this terrible fever. There are not too many people dying, which is a blessing, but you just never know who will recover and who won't.

While Bertie watches the children in the mornings, I spend time over at Daddy's house. It is devastating to see him so sick. I have never seen Daddy lie in bed—ever. He is pale and sweaty and burning up with fever. I kneel at his bedside and pray for him.

He is sixty-nine and usually in very good health. He has always been a fighter and the constant rock in my life. We haven't always been well-off, but we've never, ever gone without, and that is all because of the amazing man lying in this bed. I know we would all be crushed if we lost him, especially after just losing James. I really don't think Momma would survive it.

Each morning, I ride down to Daddy's house to sit with him, hoping he will begin to improve with each visit. Sadly, I don't see any improvement. Yesterday, I thought he might slip away as I held his hand. I pray and pray at his bedside, just knowing that God will take care of him and that he will be fine in a few days.

I was wrong.

Momma said after I left yesterday, Daddy got considerably worse and died in the middle of the night. I feel so guilty about not being there when he died, and heartbroken that I lost my daddy. My world is crumbling around me, and I don't know what to do about it. How can I live without my daddy? I cry nonstop for a whole day. I wish Rice would come home. I never needed anyone more than I need him right now. I make all kinds of deals with God. I bargain, I plead, I ask, I beg, I pray. None of these seem to work. My Rice does not come home.

In contrast to the large parties Daddy always threw with lots of people in attendance, not many people attend his funeral service. Everyone in town is either sick with the fever or nursing someone who is sick with the fever. We have a very small family service at his graveside.

When the funeral is over, I place some white daisies on his grave and whisper, "Goodbye, Daddy."

That's it. My daddy is gone.

Afterward, I can hardly function. I don't eat, I don't sleep. Thank God Martha Jane is here to help, although she's not much help. She's trying. Since she also lost her daddy, I am just grateful she is here. Bertie went back to the house to take care of Momma.

Poor Momma looks like death herself. She has lost her best friend and I am very worried about her. However, with nine children in my care, I have to let her grieve without me. I am just overwhelmed by it all.

"Momma?" Mattie calls as she enters my room.

"What, honey?" I respond.

"Have you heard anything about Daddy coming home?" she asks sadly.

"No, I haven't, Mattie. Why do you ask?"

She thinks about her answer for a moment. "It just seems like they would allow him to come home for a while, considering how bad it is around here."

I sit down on the bed and pat the quilt, inviting her to sit down as I try to explain. "Mattie, you are so bright, and I agree with you. There's nothing I want more than for your daddy to come home. But as much as we've been through, everyone else has suffered just as much. If all the men went home because everyone is having a hard time, we would lose the war and essentially lose our honor and freedom. In the big picture, freedom is more important than one person. It is more important than your uncle James or your aunt Martha. It is more important than your grandpa. Your uncle James and your grandpa would be mortified if we gave up and walked away from what we know is right, just because something is hard right now."

She is quiet for a moment, and then says, "I never thought of it that way."

"Mattie, I know what we have experienced is hard and what we've lost is very painful, but we just need to stay the course and be brave and strong. When your daddy finally comes home, we want him to be proud that we handled everything so well. Our lives will be different without your grandpa and your uncle James, but we can't just curl up into a ball and beg your daddy to come home. We have to be strong, not just for ourselves, but for Daddy."

Mattie looks at me, and a flood of emotion comes over her. Her eyes brim with tears, her lip quivers, her heart breaking.

I move closer and wrap her in my arms. As soon as she enters the safety of my embrace, the floodgates open. She sobs uncontrollable tears of grief and pain for the longest time. I hold her and stroke her hair and let her cry.

After a while, her tears subside and she falls asleep in my arms. I gently lay her on the bed and cover her with the quilt.

As I leave the room, I think that, yes, we do need to grieve, but I have children to take care of and a husband who will be coming home soon. I need to listen to my own words, and emerge from this painful sadness and get back to work taking care of the children and the store. I feel something click inside me and vow there will be no more tears.

"We need to be brave and strong," I repeat to myself.

Murfreesboro, Tennessee; December 31, 1862

The ground is hard. The air is chilly. Every night, it is pitch black out here. I haven't been able to sleep a wink. I can hear some low, quiet talking outside, an old hoot owl in the woods far away, a couple of bullfrogs croaking in the grass, and even someone snoring next to me. I wish I could sleep.

I remember the day we arrived. The land here was quite beautiful then. There were thick woods of cedar trees lining a beautiful river.

That was a month ago. Over the last three weeks, most of the trees have been used for firewood, to build makeshift cabins, and turned into poles to hold up tents. It's been raining a lot, mixed with a little snow and freezing rain. When the sun comes out in the morning, everything melts. Now this once beautiful land looks like one big, muddy pigsty. The mud is awful and the smell is even worse. God, the smell.

We were told that we would be awakened well before dawn for a mission. It must be almost that time. I'm tired. I'm anxious. I'm hungry. If we have a mission this early, there won't be time for any breakfast. Maybe some hardtack and warm canteen water and that's it.

I don't know what I'd do right now for a good, strong cup of hot coffee. We haven't had any coffee for weeks. We've been boiling chicory and peanuts instead. I would like some real coffee.

I would also like some clean clothes and some new shoes as well. I wonder if Mr. Calhoun has new shoes selling in the store. I would like some of his well-made shoes without mud on them, and with soles that aren't worn through. I would like some clothes that aren't caked in mud and sweat. I would like a chicken supper. I would like to see my wife and my children. I would like to get away from these drunken, loud men. I would like to get away from the coughing and the diseases that are spreading through our camp like wildfire. I would like to get back to my civilized store and my comfortable life, away from this godforsaken war that has gone on far too long for my taste. I should have been home months ago.

I hear them outside moving around now. I hear them all waking up and starting to stir. Someone sticks his head in my tent and says, "Rice, come on, we're meeting at the captain's tent in ten minutes."

Yeah, there is something big going on, all right. One can almost cut the tension in the air with a knife. In ten minutes, we will find out exactly what it is. I put on my coat and hat and what remains of my worn shoes, and head through the mud to the captain's tent.

"Men, you all know we have Yankees just over the river. We've heard that they plan to engage us after breakfast, but we're not going to wait for them to come across. We're going to give them a nice little surprise wake-up right now." He points to a map on the table and continues. "The Kentucky boys are going to go around this way, and the Tennessee boys are going to take them on from that direction. We will move through this way. Since it is so early, we should be able to catch most of them still asleep in their tents."

He waves his stick around the map so quickly, it is almost hard to figure out exactly where we are supposed to go.

"Any questions?" he asks.

All the men shake their heads.

"Good, let's go kick some Yankee butt. When we are finished, we will confiscate their coffee, and I'll join you in a cup," he says.

"Now you're speaking my language, Captain," I joke.

He smiles and pats me on the shoulder as I leave the tent.

We grab our muskets and revolvers and move through what remains of the dense cedar glades, up the river bank, as quiet as deer at dusk. It is still dark. I guess it must be about four or four thirty in the morning. We usually move to the sound of drum and bugle, but not on this day. Today, we are gravely quiet. As we plant ourselves behind some low limestone rocks about seven hundred yards away from the enemy, I can see about thirty campfires and a few men wandering around, but the camp is mostly quiet. It might be my imagination, but I think I smell coffee. Oh, what I wouldn't give for a cup of that. It dawns on me that there are a lot more campfires than men, so they must want us to think that their army is a lot bigger than it actually is. Why else have so many campfires?

I am uncomfortable lying on my belly so low on the ground behind eight-inch-tall limestone rocks, and I wonder why we haven't built some fortifications over the last month. Not that there are any trees left to build them with, but I wonder nonetheless. I assume we weren't planning on this attack, but since the opportunity has presented itself, we are going to take advantage of it, with or without fortifications.

When everyone gets into position, we start aiming for the men who are walking around, though when they hear the first gunshot, they crouch down, running and scurrying for their guns. I see quite a few of them fall before I ever hear one of their guns shooting back at us. For a moment, I think this is going to be an easy victory. We'll send those Yankees back home with their tails between their legs before dawn. Then we'll drink their coffee.

A few days ago, about twenty-five hundred of our Calvary boys rode all the way around the Union camp, confiscated four wagon trains, and took about a thousand Union prisoners, but we didn't get any coffee. Maybe these Yankees don't have much coffee, either.

"Well, they're not getting any today," I mumble to myself as I raise my musket and fire.

As the Yankees start to run away, someone behind us gives the rebel yell and we all follow suit. It is a mix of an Indian war cry and a gypsy scream. The Yankees probably think Indians are attacking them. We all rise from our positions and start running after them.

After we cross the freezing cold river, we pick up speed and are almost right on top of them. We are moving in and fast. Roughly ten thousand Confederate troops are raining down on their heads before breakfast. Most of those Yankees boys are running away like scared little rabbits.

"Run, rabbit, run!" I yell.

Our band starts playing "Dixie" and we hum along as we aim, fire, and reload. Occasionally, cannon fire shakes the ground, fills the air with smoke, and drowns out the band. One cannon fires so close behind me, I think my hearing will be gone for good. I am aiming at a Yankee when the cannon fires. I blink my eyes and the Yankee is gone.

One of the boys loading the cannon yells to me, "I got him for you, Rice. You go on home now."

He roars with laughter as I roll my eyes at him and wiggle my finger in my ear, gesturing that I can't hear him. He laughs louder.

Our band is now playing "My Bonnie Blue Flag" as we start moving in closer. We walk so far and so long, it seems the Yankees have all but run all the way back home. We move for a solid two miles before we catch up with them again. By the time we engage them again, it is light outside.

Our band always plays marches like "Marching Through Georgia" or "I'm a Good Ole Rebel." The Yankees bands always play songs like "Battle Hymn of the Republic." A popular song on both sides is "Home Sweet Home," but our band is not allowed to play that. The captain says the melancholy tune makes everyone homesick, and he is afraid some of the men will desert and go home. But for some reason on this cold Tennessee morning, our band starts playing that song.

Our boys always sing along, but today, the strangest thing happens. The Union boys start singing along. I can hear them singing over the gunfire. I can't believe I can hear Yankees singing, partly because they are that close, but mostly because we are in the heat of battle. Singing together seems more than bizarre to me. Then the Union band picks up on the tune and they start to play along also. Everyone is singing and for a split second, the shooting stops. For a brief moment, the cannon fire stops.

I think, how can everyone sing together and then resume shooting one another? How can everyone share this melancholy moment and take up arms again? Men on both sides are singing together like I've never heard anyone sing before. In another time, another place, we would be friends.

I stop firing and listen to everyone singing, thinking this is the most surreal moment I can remember in my life. I am lying flat on my stomach, and I lift my head to look around at the men. As I rise further and turn to look at the ones behind me, I feel a searing pain rip through my chest. I reach up to my chest and feel warm blood oozing out of a bullet wound. Damn. I optimistically think it is probably only a surface wound, and I will be all right if I can make it all the way back to camp. I can write to Mary and tell her I'm all right. I don't want her and the children to worry about me.

As I try to get to my feet and turn toward the direction of camp, I feel another hot pain go through my left temple.

I hear someone yell, "Rice, get down!"

I fall to my knees, thinking this can't possibly be the end. No, it can't be. I have a beautiful wife and wonderful children to get home to. I try to get up again, but stumble forward and fall facedown onto the ground.

"Rice!" I hear someone yell again.

I stare at the pebbles and the pine needles on the ground. Blood starts to pool under my face, turning the dirt and pebbles and pine needles a flood of bright red.

I listen as the cannons roar and the rifles fire and the band plays "Home Sweet Home," and I think of my beautiful Mary and my wonderful children—Mattie, Benjamin, Charlie, and Monroe. How lucky I am to have them.

Then slowly, everything fades from red to black.

Mr. Lincoln

Apparently Mr. Lincoln is not getting the news that the South is winning the war. Our men have been gone such a long time, but this war surely has to come to an end very soon. Back in September, the newspaper said Mr. Lincoln issued a proclamation that if the South doesn't return to the Union by January 1, 1863, he will free all of our slaves.

Today is January 1. I wonder how he plans to carry out his great threat. Is he going to come down here and take the slaves home with him? Where are they supposed to go? What are they supposed to do? I just don't know how he thinks he can make this happen.

I head over to Momma's house to have a talk with her about Daddy's slaves.

"Momma, do you think you can hang on until the boys come home?"

"I guess I can, but with our dollar declining the way it is, I don't think there is enough money to plant in the spring."

I think about that for a moment. "Well, even if you do plant, there's nowhere to sell the harvest. Those Yankees have stopped the trains and blocked the rivers. The cotton bales from last fall are still sitting in the field."

She looks out across the yard in deep contemplation.

Finally, she asks, "When do you think the boys will come home?"

"I have no idea. Rice said they'd be back by harvest, but that didn't happen. And if Mr. Lincoln is turning the war into a fight over slavery, it might get worse and be longer than we hoped. Obviously he's getting desperate and who knows what a desperate man will do."

Momma says, "You know, some of our neighbors have already released their slaves." Momma's brow wrinkles as she tries to comprehend that.

"Where are they supposed to go?" I ask, not expecting an answer.

"I don't know."

After a few minutes, I ask, "So, do you think Daddy's slaves should be freed?"

"I was thinking about it, Mary Ann. I know your daddy has tens of thousands of dollars invested in those slaves, but there's no work for them to do and very little food to feed them. I can't oversee them by myself, and with your daddy gone and your brothers off fighting, I really don't know what else to do with them."

I cringe as I ask, "Can you sell them?"

"I don't think so. I spoke to Mr. Pace and Mr. Calhoun about that, but they said no one will spend money on a slave right now with the threat of losing them looming. It's like throwing money into the creek."

I sit silently, wondering what Momma should

do. After a while, I say, "But when we win the war, everything will go back to normal, right?"

Momma shakes her head. "I don't think so. Now that the fire of abolition has been lit, it will keep burning. It won't be put out. The slaves will eventually be free, sooner or later."

After some thought I finally say, "Well, maybe you should just sell the farm and come live with me and Martha Jane."

"Oh, no, dear, you don't have the room and I wouldn't impose on you. When Rice comes home, you will need your family together as a family, without me or Martha Jane in the way. As a matter of fact, when Rice comes home, you need to send Martha Jane back here."

I rack my brain to come up with another solution. Momma interrupts my train of thought. "Why don't you and Martha Jane and the children come live here with me? I have plenty of room."

"That's a great offer, Momma, and the children would love it, but I can't leave the store. Rice loves being a merchant and I need to hang on until he comes home."

"Well, I guess since we can't come up with a plan, we'll just have to leave it in God's hands." She pauses for a minute. "You know, a couple of the men offered to help run the farm until the boys come home, but I just don't know."

"What did you tell them?"

"I told them I would think about it and let them know when I decide what I want to do," she replies.

After a few days of thinking about it, Momma

tells me she has decided to let all the slaves go. There is no place to sell them. There is no work for them to do. And at this point, there is little food to feed them. A few of them stay on the land, wondering where they should go. Momma doesn't say anything to them. She lets them stay. Bertie and five-year-old Tony Washington are the only two who decide not to go.

Tony's parents both died of the fever a few weeks earlier, and Bertie decided to raise Tony as her own. Bertie asks Momma if she can stay on the plantation with little Tony. Momma is happy to let them stay and happy to have the company. She loves Bertie, but I don't know if she ever told her so.

Bad to Worse

A few weeks into the New Year, I receive word that Rice's sisters Harriet and Mary Louise are both sick with the fever. I know it is the sisterly thing to do to go over and help them, and I want to do so, but I am really coming to my wits' end with all this sickness and death. For my own sanity, I need to stay home with my children and James's children and get some rest. I decide that if their husbands get sick, I will go help, but if not, they will have to rely on other family. I am exhausted.

It is a dreary, rainy, thundering afternoon. The children are curled up on chairs and on the floor, reading or sitting at the table playing a game by lamplight. I ask Mattie, now fourteen years old, to help Martha Jane keep an eye on the little ones while I go in the bedroom to lie down for a few minutes. My head is pounding and I feel a little ill. I crawl into bed with baby Monroe Franklin and snuggle up next to him, smelling his sweet head of baby hair. I am glad to have a few quiet moments with him. He is getting so big, so fast. He is already ten months old and trying to walk to keep up with the older children. He is such a good baby. I wish desperately that Rice would come home and see him. Rice hasn't been a part of Monroe's life for such a long time. He hasn't even seen the child since he was two months old. Monroe and I fall asleep snuggled up next to each other under a warm quilt, listening to the sound of the rain tapping on the roof.

I wake a while later to the sound of the children laughing in the other room. I love to hear their laughter filling the house and I smile, thinking that for right now in this one small moment, everything is okay. I also notice that I am feeling better. It must have just been an ordinary headache plaguing me. I look toward the window and notice it is pretty dim outside, so it is either starting to get dusk or it is still cloudy and rainy. With no sunlight to judge by, I have no idea how long I was asleep. I figure the children are probably getting hungry or will be hungry soon, so I'd better get up and get some supper cooking.

I reach down to stroke the soft head of my baby boy. He is hot. Oh, no. I hope he doesn't have the fever everyone else has, but I'm sick to my stomach thinking that's exactly what he has. I sit up and start to take off his shirt. He stirs and whimpers a little but does not fully wake. I call to the other room for Mattie to bring me a wet cloth to wipe him down with.

When Mattie brings it to me, she looks pale and ill also.

"Are you not feeling well?" I ask her.

"No, ma'am, I feel tired, and I have chills and a little headache."

"Come over here," I motion to her. I reach up and touch her forehead. She has a fever, too. "Go to bed right now. I will be in there in a few minutes," I tell her.

What in the world am I going to do with a house full of sick children? This is going to be a nightmare. I wash Monroe Franklin to cool him down, and I place him in his crib in only his diaper. Then I head to the next room to check on Mattie.

As I pass through the parlor, heading to Mattie's room, Martha Jane yells up the stairs, "Mary, there's a gentleman here. He says he has to see you."

I poke my head in the bedroom door and tell Mattie I will check on her in a few minutes. I return to my room to get my day cap. I smooth down my wrinkled dress and head downstairs.

When I reach the bottom of the stairs, I see him. I do not recognize his face, but I recognize his clothing. He is a Confederate soldier. He is standing in the open doorway of the store with the gray, cloudy sky at his back. He is dressed in a wrinkled gray uniform with a dirty yellow cummerbund. His trousers have holes in them, with mud caked around the bottoms of his pant legs. His jacket is missing some buttons, and he looks quite thin and weary. He is wearing shoes that are covered in red Mississippi mud and probably have no soles on the bottom. He is holding his tattered hat and a piece of paper in his dirty hands.

"Hello, sir, what can I do for you?" I ask as I approach.

"Hello, ma'am." He nods. "Are you Mrs. Carpenter?"

"Yes, I am. And who are you, may I ask?"

"Private Joseph Brown, ma'am. Captain asked me to deliver the latest casualty list to you in person." He holds the folded piece of paper toward me and looks down at the floor, like a child in trouble for doing something wrong.

"Why are you delivering this? It usually comes by a mail carrier," I ask as I reach for the paper. I look at the boy's face. He nervously avoids my eyes and keeps staring at the floor.

"Why are you delivering this to me?" I repeat.

"I promised I would. I'm sorry, ma'am. Goodbye, ma'am," he murmurs, and backs out the open door.

I look at the piece of paper in my hand for a long time, wondering if I can open it. I don't know whose names are on this paper, but I suspect the worst, and I don't want to read it. My eyes sting with tears as I dread a simple piece of paper. I try to unfold it, but my hands are shaking, so I stop and hold it to my chest. I take a deep breath.

Martha Jane stands behind me, not saying a word or making a sound.

"Martha Jane, will you please go upstairs and mind the children for a few minutes?" I ask her.

She nods and quietly heads up the stairs.

I walk outside across the wooden porch and down the two stone steps onto the ground. I walk across the dirt road that is now filled with puddles of red mud from the rain. I keep walking straight ahead. I walk into the overgrown field across the road. I walk with purpose, with determination, like I have somewhere important to go. I want to run. I want to run away and never come back. I keep walking.

In the middle of the field, the thunder sounds above my head. I stop and look up at the ominous clouds that are almost as threatening as the piece of paper I hold in my hand. My hands are shaking as I slowly unfold it and smooth it open. My stomach feels like it has a hole in it. My eyes fill with tears. My hands are now trembling so violently, I almost can't read it. The name at the top is the only name I see.

"*Carpenter, Rice Benjamin: killed in battle 31 December, 41st Mississippi Infantry, Co C.*"

Drops of water fall onto the page, but I can't tell if they are raindrops or teardrops. Even God Himself is crying.

All I've wanted the last seven months is for my husband to come home and hold me and tell me everything will be all right. All I've done for the last seven months is managed the store and the family, and I've waited—waited for Rice to come home. I've waited and I've prayed and I've done everything possible in preparation for him to come home to me.

I've dreamed of his homecoming. I've dreamed of taking up our lives where we left off. I've imagined us having more children. I've wished for his arms around me. I've seen his blue eyes in my dreams so often and heard his laughter ringing in my head over and over. I've pictured seeing his beautiful Carpenter smile as he runs up the road and takes me in his arms. My heart always feels like bursting at the thought of seeing him again. I've imagined our happy reunion hundreds of times.

Now what? There will be no homecoming. There will be no funeral. There will be no body. There will be no goodbye. It's just over. My heart is ripping out of my chest in a pain I can't even try to describe. My future is gone. My past is gone. My present is gone. Everything is gone. It all died with Rice.

I stand in the middle of the field in a blinding thunderstorm, holding a wet piece of paper that is all that is left of my husband, and I scream at the top of my lungs.

January 31, 1863

I hear that Rice's sisters, Harriet and Mary Louise, are both getting worse with the fever, but in taking care of my own children, Monroe and Mattie, and my niece and nephew, Necie and Allen John, who have also come down with the fever, I don't have the energy or the time to go and help. I pray for Harriet and Mary Louise and hope they will recover quickly.

Shortly after dawn on January 31st, Harriet's husband, William, comes to the store. We are not open yet, so he knocks on the locked door. By the time I get downstairs and reach the door, William is climbing back on his horse to leave. I am just in time to stop him and ask him to come inside. He looks tired and sad. I can just imagine how tired he must be, taking care of Harriet and their four children by himself, because I am also that tired. He probably hasn't had a good meal or a good night's sleep in a couple of weeks. I feel a little guilty for not going over there to help him, but I remind myself I have sick children upstairs, and Harriet and Mary Louise have other family who can pitch in.

After I invite him in, I offer him some coffee and breakfast. He says he is not hungry but will take me up on the coffee. As we sit down at the table with our cups of hot coffee, I ask him what the reason is for his visit.

"Mary Ann, I don't even know how to tell you this."

"Tell me what, William? What is it?"

"Harriet and Mary Louise both died yesterday."

I feel like the air has been sucked out of the room. When will it stop? How many more will die of war or fever? How much more can we possibly take? I feel so sorry for William. I also feel sorry for Rice's parents. They lost their granddaughter Martha three months ago to the fever. Then they lost their son in the war. Now they have lost two daughters at the same time. I am shocked and totally numb. I don't think I even have any tears left to cry for my sisters-in-law.

After I absorb what William just told me, he continues, "Mary Ann, I know you are busy with the children and you are grieving your lost husband, but I need to ask you a favor. I don't know who else to ask."

"If I can help, you know I will. What is it?"

I reach out to touch his hand.

William looks down at his coffee and exhales all the air out of his lungs. I don't know what he's going to say, but I see that it is very difficult for him to ask for help. He is a very proud man. For a moment, I think he is going to ask me to take in his four children, and I panic. Then I think there is no way he would impose to that extent. Would he? I hold my breath.

"With all the deaths around here recently, there are no coffins available anywhere for my wife and her sister. I know it is right and Christian to bury them the right way, but with this awful inflation and the lack of money to buy coffins and the lack of supplies and manpower to make them, I just don't see how it will be possible to find two coffins by tomorrow."

He pauses for a moment to collect his courage to continue.

I don't carry coffins in the store, so I have no idea where this conversation is headed, but I am relieved he is not asking me to take in his children. I sit silently and wait for him to continue.

"What I am wondering is if you have any material in the store that we could use to make burial shrouds?" he asks, staring at his coffee cup.

"Material? Yes, I have material."

"The problem is, I can't pay you now, but I will pay you as soon as I am able."

He quickly takes a drink of his coffee, like he is glad to wash the taste of asking for help out of his mouth. The thought of Harriet and Mary Louise not having a proper burial brings tears to my eyes. How can things have gotten this bad? How can everything be so rotten that a man can't even find a coffin to bury his wife properly? The store is dwindling down to nothing. We are running out of just about everything and have no money to buy supplies. We are out of all spices and flour and sugar. We are out of guns and almost out of ammunition. We have very little canned fruit and vegetables, and the children are eating those before they can be displayed on the shelves. But we have material. We have plenty of material. The last thing I care about right now is whether or not William can pay me for it. Regardless of my own troubles, William and I are family, and we are obviously stuck in this mess together, so I go downstairs and gather all the material I have and give it to William. We are certainly not going to make cotillion dresses out of any of it anytime soon, and no one is going to spend money on it when they need to buy food for their children. I figure this is probably the best use of it, and I am happy to help William.

Harriet and Mary Louise's funerals follow the next day, but I can't attend. I have four sick children in my household. Allen John and Necie seem to be doing a little better. Mattie is about the same. But my poor Monroe Franklin is not doing well at all. It crosses my mind a hundred times a day to write to Rice and beg him to come home and be with his son. Then over and over like a lightning bolt to my heart, I remember that Rice will not be coming home again. Rice will not be coming home ever. I feel so lost and lonely and don't know what I am supposed to do now. I just want this sickness to end and I want this damn war to be over, though I don't know what good that will do now that Rice is gone.

For the next two days and nights, I sit on the bed and hold Monroe Franklin and cry my eyes out. And I pray. I pray like I have never prayed before. I pray for healing for the children. I pray for strength for myself. I pray that this is all a bad dream and Rice will walk in the door and take me in his arms.

As the sun rises on February 3rd, I hold my beautiful Monroe Franklin in my arms as he takes his last breath.

Monroe

If my heart was not broken from losing my daddy and my dear Rice, it certainly is shattered into little tiny splinters now. If I didn't feel so sad, I would think I didn't even have a heart left in my chest. I cannot stop crying, and I have to remind myself every few minutes to breathe. I think of Momma losing two sons at the same time, and once again, I wonder how she made it through the pain. Losing a brother is bad. Losing a father is bad. Losing a husband is bad. Losing a child? I just don't know how to survive this. Somehow I continue breathing. I think Bertie and Martha Jane help with the children, the cooking, and the store, but I don't really know for sure. I can't remember one moment to the next. I don't know how, but each moment just comes and goes and I am still alive.

The reverend comes over the following morning to talk about the funeral service. I haven't even thought about that. I haven't thought about anything at all except that this just can't be happening.

All I know is I have a dead son upstairs wrapped in a blanket in his cradle, and I keep reminding myself to breathe.

Reverend Jones says, "Mary, there are no coffins at all in the entire county. How would you like to bury little Monroe?"

I don't know what to say or how to answer the question. I think of William asking me for material and ask the reverend if we can bury Monroe in a shroud. I don't have any material left, but I guess I can take apart a dress or use a quilt.

He says, "Yes, of course. We will do what we have to do."

After he leaves, I think about the lack of coffins. I think about the lack of food and supplies. I think about the lack of men to run farms and the lack of carpenters and saw-mill operators and businesses owners. I'm devastated over the lack of a husband and a father to help me get through this. I feel angrier and angrier at the entire situation. At the North. At the South. At the whole country. Why did the North have to start pushing us around? Why do the proud men of the South see war as the only option? Why is this fever killing people? Why does my baby boy not have a suitable coffin? It's bad enough to lose a child, but to not have the means to bury him properly is just too much to bear.

I run out the front door of the store, cross the street, and run through the field. I run until I can't run anymore. When I eventually stop running, I bend over with my hands on my knees and gulp for air. After I finally catch my breath, I scream as loud and as long as I can. Then I fall down in the tall, half-dead grass and sob. I sob for my little Monroe. I sob for myself.

After a while, I compose myself and head back toward home, knowing that I need to prepare a shroud for tomorrow's funeral. I am still infuriated that I don't have a proper coffin to bury my son in, but when it is all said and done, being angry will not fix anything. I resign myself to the fact that I will have to make do with what I have. As I sluggishly walk back to the store, I wipe stray tears from my cheeks. When I reach the road, I stop and look at the front of the store.

"There isn't much here for me anymore," I think. "Maybe we should move to Momma's house."

I take a deep breath and walk across the road. When I step up the two steps onto the porch, I hear someone coming up the road. I stop and turn to see who it is. It is William in a wagon pulled by a single horse. He comes to a stop in front of the store and climbs down. There is something a little different about him. He is standing taller. He is moving fast. He is like a man on a mission. I look at his face. His temples are throbbing. His jaw is tense. His skin is red. He is angry. I don't understand.

"Mary, I am so sorry about your baby," he says as he walks toward me and steps up on the porch.

"Thank you, William. It is very kind of you to come all this way."

He gives me a quick, tense hug.

When he releases me, he says, "Well, I came to give you something. I made something for you."

He takes my hand and leads me from the steps of the store to the rear of the wagon.

I don't know what to say. A gift? It is highly unlikely William would give me a gift. And the timing could not be more wrong. I have no idea what is going on here.

When we reach the back of the wagon, he lifts a tarp and shows me what he has done. I gasp and raise my hand to my mouth.

"I started on it the minute I heard what happened," he explains, pulling the tarp off and crumpling it up in a ball.

"How did you do this?"

"I pulled the boards off my barn," he responds with an edge in his voice I can't place.

Sitting in the back of his wagon is the smallest, most beautifully hand-carved coffin I have ever seen. It has ivy vines carved into the corners, and on the top is carved "MFC."

I move my hand down to my chest as I try to catch my breath. My eyes fill with tears. "William, why would you do something like this?" I ask.

"Please accept this as my thank you for the material you gave me. I can't pay you money right now, but I can do this for you."

He picks up the tiny coffin and carries it into the store.

I follow him in as he moves quickly and continues talking. "I have also just reached the end of my rope with all that we've been through. I'm just not going to sit back and do nothing. You deserve to be able to bury your son properly, and I am going to make sure that happens. We can't give Monroe a long life, but we can at least bury him the way he deserves."

He's angry. That's what it is. I can feel his rage and think he has so much more to say, but he stops and I don't want to push him.

He places the small coffin on the floor near

the stairs and turns to me. "I will come back in the morning with the wagon and carry you and Monroe's coffin to the cemetery. Do you need help putting him in here?"

I shake my head.

"All right, then. I'll see you tomorrow," he says. He gives me a nod and heads out the door.

I am speechless. I didn't even say thank you. No one in my life has ever done anything this special for me before. As I hear William's horse trotting away, I sit down on the floor next to the tiny coffin. I cry for an hour. I cry tears of sadness for Monroe Franklin and tears of gratitude for William Jolly.

The next morning, we bury my son. The sky is blue and the birds are singing in the trees. There is a gentle breeze blowing through the treetops. It is like any other beautiful day in Lauderdale County, except that my son is dead. I look around at the funeral and see that there are very few people in attendance due to everyone still fighting the fever.

Funerals aren't like they used to be. Friends and family used to come from all over to pay their respects and share food and fellowship. Now, with so many folks sick and dying, a scant few people come to any service, and the few who do come immediately leave to go back to their homes. There is no food to share. There is no time or energy for fellowship.

Following the funeral, Bertie walks the children back to the store. William offers to drive me back, but I tell him I'd rather stay at the cemetery for a while and then walk home. He is now a widower with four children to care for; he has more to do than cart me around. He has certainly done enough for me already. After everyone leaves the cemetery, I sit quietly on the green grass at the foot of the newly dug grave containing my baby boy. My mother comes up behind me and sits down next to me.

"How did you do it?" I ask her without looking at her.

"How did I do what?"

"How did you get through losing Stephen and William at the same time?" I stare at the mound of red dirt.

"I don't know. You just get out of bed in the morning and you keep going."

"But it just hurts so much," I sob, wiping tears from my cheek.

"I know it does, Mary." She pauses, letting me cry for a few minutes. When the wave of grief subsides, she continues. "Everything will be okay. You'll see. God's will be done," she says, patting my arm.

I stop crying and look at her.

"Okay? *Okay*?" I raise my voice and pull my arm away from her touch. "No, Momma, everything will not be okay. Everything will never be okay ever again. I brought that little boy into this world to grow up and become a young man. I wanted him to learn to walk and talk, to learn to read and write, to learn to fish and hunt and someday raise his own family. I brought him into this world to love his parents and his brothers and his sister and God. I brought him into this world to help take care of his grandparents in their old age. I gave life to him so he could grow up to be a strong, loving, and honorable man like his father."

Tears fill my eyes at the thought of Rice, but I quickly shake them off. I can't allow myself to think of Rice right now or I might just curl up in a little ball and die myself.

I continue, "You think it was God's will that Monroe die at the age of one? One, Momma, he was one!"

I look up to the sky and rise to my feet.

My voice grows louder and stronger than I ever remember it being as I scream at the sky. "Why? Why did you take him from me? Why? He was just a little baby. He never did anything wrong. He didn't deserve this. I don't deserve this! None of us deserve *any of this*!" I stop for a moment and stare at the cloudless sky as if waiting for an answer. I stand there, angry, waiting, tears streaming down my cheeks.

Finally I look down at my mother, who is still sitting on the grass, staring straight ahead with silent tears pouring down her face.

"Momma, why is this happening? What could possibly be in it for God? Or for us? First James and Martha, then Daddy and Rice, and now Monroe. And what about Timothy? Did our Timothy die alone in a hospital? We haven't heard from him in over six months. Is he dead, too? He always hated to be alone. Did he die alone, Momma? I swear I can't take one more minute of sickness and death. I'm sick of the fever. I'm sick of the war. I'm sick of being hungry. I'm sick of going without. And I'm sick of carrying the whole god-damn world on my shoulders. I'm sick of all of it. I can't take one more thing! Period!"

A month later, Momma dies of the fever.

Martin Warren

By March, the store is completely empty except for the occasional visitor who comes in to check the casualty list. The house feels so empty to me, knowing that Rice is gone, that James and Martha aren't going to stop by, and that Daddy isn't just down the road. My arms feel empty without baby Monroe to fill them, and my heart feels empty without my husband's love. But I clean and cook and take all of the children to school every day.

The days drag on endlessly. I pray every day to hear word from my brothers, but there is none. William works sunup until sundown on his farm. Bertie lives alone on Daddy's property. She moved into the old slave house at Daddy's and minds little orphan, Tony Washington. Mattie, who recently turned fifteen, is really stepping up to help with the younger children when they aren't in school. She will make a great mother someday.

Allen John and Benjamin have suddenly taken an interest in hunting and like to disappear during the early morning hours, happily returning later in the day with a wild turkey or a couple of ducks for supper.

When there is no school, William brings his two youngest children over almost daily. Cornelia is eight and little Bud is four. I mind them while

William works on his farm. He is busy trying to get the fields ready to plant in a few weeks.

His older daughters, Virginia and Mary Eliza, who are seventeen and fourteen, stay home to manage the housekeeping so we seldom see them, but they do occasionally come over with their dad for supper. On most evenings, when William returns to pick up his children, he brings fruit from his trees and vegetables from last fall's harvest that he stored. We suddenly have enough food every night for supper, and we usually have a full house with Martha Jane, William, me, and at least nine of the eleven children. By the grace of God, we seldom go to bed hungry anymore.

In early April, Martha Jane receives a letter from Company H, 8th Mississippi Infantry. That is the company her husband is with, and I am expecting the worst. I stand facing her with dreaded anticipation as she opens the letter.

Dear Mrs. Warren,

I regret to inform you of the death of Private Martin V. Warren. Private Warren was wounded severely in the face on December 31, 1862, at the battle in Murfreesboro, Tennessee. He died of his injuries on February 20 of this year.

Our heartfelt condolences go out to you and his family, and our sincerest thanks go out to him for his service. His records show he has no personal effects to send home.

Sincerely,
Capt. James Lasley

Martha Jane finishes reading the letter and her face lights up with relief, even a touch of happiness. I don't understand her reaction. Is he coming home? What has happened?

I ask her, "What is it?"

"He's dead," she replies and hands me the letter.

"What? Who? Martin?" I ask.

"Yes, Martin. He's dead." She runs up the stairs.

I'm completely confused by the combination of the disturbing news and the smile on her face. I walk outside with the letter and sit down on the front steps. I begin to read the letter. When I get to the part about him being wounded in the face, I think I might be sick. When I read the part about "December 31, 1862, at the battle in Murfreesboro," I jump up and run to the side of the porch and throw up.

That was the same battle Rice was killed in. Oh my God. It must have been so bloody and I can't believe Martin survived six weeks with injuries to his face. He must have been in so much pain. Poor Martin. All of the horrible feelings of receiving the news of Rice's death flood back to me.

I sit back down on the steps, trying to catch my breath and willing myself not to cry. My sister comes bouncing out of the store, holding a yellow dress up to her body.

"What do you think of trimming all these sleeves off and reworking the neckline to come down to here?" she asks, moving her free hand around the dress in demonstration.

"Martha Jane, that color is hardly appropriate

for a grieving widow," I say quietly.

"Who's grieving?" she asks, looking like I just slapped her or that she thinks I am the most ignorant person in the world.

"You read this letter, right? Martin is dead," I say, shaking the piece of paper in my hand toward her.

"Yes," she starts slowly, "and that means I am no longer a married woman. I can now go to dances and barbecues and have some fun. So, what about the dress?"

She holds the dress close to her and spins around. I just stare at her in disbelief. The news of Martin's death is devastating. The reaction from Martha Jane leaves me speechless.

Receiving no response from me about the dress, she sighs, shrugs, and goes back inside.

Martin's brother comes around shortly after we receive the news of his death and tries to get Martha Jane to help settle Martin's estate, but she refuses to have any part of it.

Martin didn't own a lot, only a small piece of land and a couple horses, but after almost two years of being married to a stranger, Martha Jane is just relieved it is over and does not want to deal with Martin's family or his estate. Martin's brother ends up selling the items and gives Martha Jane the money.

After a marriage that amounted to nothing more than a piece of paper, a union Martha Jane viewed as a jail sentence, all she knows is that she is finally free. She can finally stop being a good wife in the eyes of the community and go out and have a little fun. She refuses to mourn. She refuses to wear black. She immediately takes her brightest-colored dresses apart, sews them into the latest styles, and is ready to go out on the town.

The only thing stopping her is the fact there are no eligible men to go out with. All of the young men have gone off to war. That leaves only old men and a few young ones who have returned on wooden crutches or with an armless shirtsleeve pinned to their chests.

None of these potential suitors interest Martha Jane. She has delusions of being a full Southern belle, with a plantation house and a lot of servants so she can sit around and fan herself all day and attend parties in the evenings. I guess she doesn't realize those days of balls and parties are long gone, and they are not coming back for a long, long time — if ever.

She flits around the store, humming and dancing. She checks her hair every five minutes in the mirror. She uses the last of the ribbon and lace from the store to re-trim her old bonnets. And suddenly, she has a big interest in running the store. She wants to be downstairs in plain view if anyone comes in. Nobody does, but she stays in sight just in case.

As frustrated as I am with her humming and dancing, I have to admit it is a breath of fresh air to see someone happy. I just didn't realize how sullen we have all been for such a long time. We have all endured more than any person should be allowed to. Who knows? Maybe Martha Jane's happy attitude will be contagious and things will start to turn around for the better.

1864

After an uneventful summer, a dismal harvest, and an empty, melancholy Christmas season, there is word that danger is brewing in the state of Mississippi. In January, we hear that General Sherman of the Union Army is heading east from Brandon on his way to destroy Meridian's railways, and he is bringing what appears to be the whole damn Union Army.

If his troops are marching toward Meridian, our little community stands right in his path. The rumors are that the Yankees are looting towns along their way. They are stealing food, horses, and livestock, and burning buildings, barns, cotton gins, and the unsold cotton bales that sit idle in the fields. They are looting homes, terrorizing residents, and taking whatever their rotten Yankee hearts desire. Then they are burning the homes down.

It has taken a long, long time, but finally the war is coming directly toward us. Unfortunately we have very few men left in town to fight the Yankees off.

We know we have to do something but we don't know what, so we meet at the church to come up with a plan.

One of the elderly men says, "We know the direction they will be coming from — the west side of our creek—so the first thing we need to do is burn down Perry Bridge. They won't be able to get to us without that bridge."

One of the other men nods in agreement. "Yes, they will have to go at least ten miles in either direction to cross that creek, and they're not going to waste time doing that if they're on their way to Meridian, so that will probably work."

We set out immediately, lay brush under the wooden bridge, and set it ablaze.

Our plan works. Our creek saves us. The Yankees stay on the west side of the creek and follow it south to Meridian. However, after they sack Meridian, they are apparently given orders to take the surrounding towns. They come back up on the east side of the creek, and this time they invade our little community in droves. There is absolutely nothing we can do to stop them, outside of joining the war effort and killing the scoundrels. They terrorize our residents. They burn down our barns. They invade our homes, looking for food and treasure.

I can hear Charlie screaming for me as he runs up the road. He flies in the front door of the store, shouting that the Union Army is coming down the street. Oh, no, here we go. Apparently I am now in the middle of this war. Unfortunately, on this day, I have all of the children with me: my three, William's four, and James's five.

I order the boys to run to the field in back and chase the hog and the horse into the woods. I order the girls to take every jug, every crock, and every jar of food from the store and the cellar, put them in the attic, barricade the door, and stay there. Then I load my rifle. I'll be damned if I'm going to let these disgraceful, plundering Yankees ruin my life any more than they already have. And I will kill every last one of them before I let them harm the children. When the Yankees arrive, I will be more than ready for them.

I watch for them out the front window of the store. My palms are sweating. My heart is pounding out of my chest. My breathing is heavy. I can also feel my anger rising like flames from the very depths of Hell. My hands are shaking, though I don't know if it is from fear or rage. I can hear them coming before I can see them. Their horses are clomping on the dry road and there is a jingling sound from their spurs and saddles. Sure enough, they stop right in front of my store. There are three of them on horseback dressed in their blue uniforms. They are filthy and unshaven and a bit thin and weary. I slowly emerge through the doorway onto the wooden front porch with my loaded rifle in my hands.

"What do you want?" I yell to the Yankees.

"Do you have any food here?" one of them asks, though it sounds more like a demand than a question.

"No, I don't have any food," I say, surprised at the sound of the strength in my own voice even though my statement is a bold lie.

"Is your husband home?" the second one asks.

"No. You already killed him," I reply, with venom in my tone that would scare off any other man, but they don't move.

"Is there a man of the house here?" the third one asks.

"No, there are no men here, just me." I raise my gun slightly.

"You need to put that gun away, ma'am. We just want some food. We're not here to hurt anyone. You have to have some kind of food in that store," the first one says with a cocky smile on his unshaven face, as he climbs down from his horse. He removes his dusty hat and takes a couple steps toward me.

"I already told you, I don't have any food," I say slowly without raising my voice. I do, however, raise my gun to my shoulder and point it squarely at the man's face. The two Yankees still on horseback put their hands on their pistols.

The man on the ground stops moving and holds up his free hand to the other two to keep them from drawing their weapons. Again, he starts to move toward me.

I cock the hammer. Again, he stops.

We seem to be at a stalemate. But what he doesn't know is that the rage inside me will have no trouble blowing his damn head off. We stare each other directly in the eye and neither of us moves.

Suddenly, there is a gunshot from behind the Yankees. All three of the men draw their weapons and spin around, but none of them know exactly which way to turn. My son Benjamin appears from around one corner of the store with a pistol pointing at the man in front of me. My nephew Allen John appears from around the other corner at the exact same time, with his rifle pointing at one of the men on horseback. Mr. Calhoun comes out from his hiding place behind a tree on the other side of the road, his rifle aimed at the second man on horseback. Mr. Pace appears from behind the shed next to the store, aiming at the man standing on the ground.

All of our guns are pointing directly at the Yankees. They know they are surrounded and they don't like it one bit. It seems as if everyone freezes for a moment as the Yankees grasp their predicament.

The man on the ground, in a desperate move, quickly spins around and points his gun at me like he is trying to frighten me into dropping my gun.

William bursts through the doorway of the store behind me with his gun over my shoulder, aiming right at the Yankees' head.

"I wouldn't do that if I were you," William growls in a voice I have never heard before. "You boys need to move along now."

After a few moments that seem like an hour, the Yankee on the ground slowly holsters his gun, puts his hat back on his head, and lifts both hands in surrender as he backs up to his horse.

"We were just looking for something to eat. We didn't mean no harm," he stammers.

The men on horseback holster their weapons. None of us lower our weapons. None of us move. The man on the ground climbs back up on his horse, and the three of them ride off as fast as lightning.

After the men ride off, William reaches in front of me and takes the loaded rifle out of my trembling hands. I'm shaking and in shock. I stand frozen in sheer terror, thinking of what could have happened.

"Are you all right?" William asks softly.

"I don't know. I think so," I say, hearing the quiver in my voice.

I look up at him. "Why are you here?"

"Right place at the right time." He smiles.

William hands our weapons to Mr. Pace and Mr. Calhoun, who have joined us on the porch, and then he wraps his arms around me.

"It's all over. It's all over," he repeats as he holds me in his arms.

I start to cry. I'm not sure why. William holds me. He doesn't let go.

That evening, William and I hold vigil on the front porch, with a fire burning in the yard and our rifles loaded. We wait for the Yankees to return, but fortunately, they never do. While we sit and wait, we talk of the hard times we are all enduring, and of the war and what kind of future we might have.

William has a good farm, a lovely house, and four beautiful children. He says since three of his four children are girls and he is obviously short on boys to help with the farm, he is hoping the farm can be profitable enough so he can pay some laborers to help plant and harvest this coming year.

"Thank you for helping me with the children," he says. "Men can't raise babies. It's just not man's work. I didn't realize how much a man needs a woman to raise the children so he can work on the farm."

I say, "You're welcome." I don't reply to the rest of his statement. I know it is all true, but I don't know what he is going to do about it.

I rock in my chair as I look out across the field

and admire the full moon and the stars. The silence of the night is only interrupted by the crickets and the occasional bullfrog croaking.

After a few minutes of silence between us, he asks, "Mary, why are you hanging on to this store?"

I try to think of an answer to give him. I feel a storm of grief well up inside of me as the reality of my situation hits me. I didn't realize until this moment that I keep myself busy to avoid thinking about it. I haven't allowed myself time to dwell on all that has happened or what the future might hold. Until now. Tears fill my eyes. I can't breathe for a moment. I try to compose myself so I can speak.

"This was Rice's dream. I tried my best to make it successful so when he returned from the war, he would be proud of me."

A sob catches in the back of my throat. I try not to cry, but tears come anyway. William sits quietly next to me and lets me work through my grief as the flood-gates open.

After a few minutes, the wave of grief passes and I take a deep breath.

I whisper through my tears, "He's not coming back."

William reaches over and gently puts his hand on my shoulder. I feel comforted by his touch and his tenderness.

After I pull myself together, I confess, "I guess I really don't know what else to do. I am trying to raise these children by myself, and I don't have the land or the help to farm, so until this moment, I thought the store was probably the best place. I guess I'm just like you in that I'm alone and really don't know how to make it on my own."

"Mary, I know you can trade goods in the store for food, but now that there is so little merchandise left, and I assume you're not making any money to purchase new supplies, how are you going to feed your children?" William pauses to let that question sink in.

It doesn't need to sink in very far. Little does he know how many nights we have gone to bed hungry. He continues, "You know, I have an idea. I have a good farm. I can help you feed your children. I've always loved them and I think they love me, too."

"Of course they do."

"As much as you need someone to help you, I need someone to help me, too," he says. "Why don't you and the children move out to my farm?"

"William, I, well, what about the store?" I ask, though in my heart I already know the answer.

"What about it? There's nothing left here for you. And you just said it was Rice's dream, not yours. What's your dream, Mary?"

"If I could have a dream, I guess it would be that this awful war never happened."

I pause and stare at the fireflies across the road in the tall grass. I know that an imaginary world is not what William is asking me, so I try to bring my thoughts back to reality.

After some careful thought, I say, "I guess my dream is to raise happy, healthy children; to take care of a home and a husband; and to get through this terrible war the best way I can."

A few minutes of silence pass between us

before William speaks again.

"I can give you all of those things, Mary. I can take care of your children. I can give you a home. I can stay by your side until this dreadful war is over, and long after that. I think for the sake of everyone involved, you should think about abandoning the store, and you and the children should move to my farm. I guess to make it all proper, we should probably get married. I know it's a lot to take in, but promise me you'll think about it."

"William, are you asking me to marry you?" I ask, stunned.

"Yeah, I guess I am." He sounds as if he is as surprised as I. I don't look at him, but I can hear the smile in his voice. He's proud that he came up with a solution to both our dilemmas.

We sit quietly for a long time while we contemplate the idea.

Finally, I break the silence.

"You know what I think, William? I don't pretend that it will be easy for me to walk away from here, but I think you are absolutely right. For the sake of everyone involved, I think we should get married and I should become Mrs. William Jolly."

Within a few days, Sherman's troops vacate Meridian, and William and I ride into the devastated town in search of the justice of the peace. We get married in the courthouse — or what's left of it.

A New Start

The move to William's farm has all of the children filled with excitement. My children love their uncle William, now their stepfather, and they love their cousins, now their stepsiblings. Everyone is so happy to be moving in together, one can just feel the delight in the air.

Just as I told William, I do find it very difficult to walk away from the store, but I have to face the truth that it was Rice's dream, not mine. I also have to face the painful reality that Rice is never coming home. So I hold my head high, fight back the tears, and put a smile on my face for the benefit of everyone around me.

On our final trip to the farm with the wagon full of furniture, I surprisingly and gratefully begin to feel a huge weight lifting off my shoulders with every mile we travel. The sun is shining. The children are happy. William is smiling. I am no longer alone, and I know my children will be well cared for. I no longer need to worry about how to feed or clothe them. I now have a partner to help me. I now have William — my husband. I glance over at him driving the wagon and admire his strong arms and his able hands leading the horses. He catches me looking at him and we smile at each other.

William and Harriet had five children, but

one of them died at an early age. The children he still has at home are three beautiful girls — Virginia, Mary Eliza, Cornelia, who are now eighteen, fifteen, and nine; and the cutest little boy named Bud, who is five years old. The boy's given name is William James Jolly, but everyone calls him Bud.

My Charlie and James's little Necie, who are now both six, love to play with Bud, and I can tell by watching the trio that they are going to be nothing but trouble. I smile at the anticipation of what they will be up to next. I'm going to have to stay a step ahead of these three.

William's eldest, Virginia is only two years older than my Mattie, but she has a serious romance going with James White, so James is also at the house constantly. We have a house full of smiles and laughter, and I treasure every moment of it. There is nothing in the world more precious than having family around. I actually find myself laughing and smiling for the first time in a very, very long time.

When Virginia and James announce they are to be married, we all have a busy and happy time planning their wedding. Virginia and I scrounge up some wool, weave it into material, and dye it with berries to make her the most beautiful wedding dress. The material transforms into a soft pink shade, the same color as low-hanging clouds at sunset. The dress is very lightweight, but we have to put so many crinolines underneath to plump out the bottom that it ends up weighing a ton.

The front is trimmed with a V-shaped black ribbon, and it has pagoda sleeves with the same black ribbon on the edges. We spend hours and hours painstakingly embroidering bold white daisies on the black ribbon. The first time she tries the dress on, I think it is absolutely stunning, and she looks gorgeous in it. Instead of a day cap and a veil, we buck tradition and make her a daisy-covered cap. I think her father will melt when he sees her in it for the first time.

In the weeks leading up to Virginia's wedding, Martha Jane is in rare form. Two days before the wedding, while I am preparing food for the party, Martha Jane bounces into the kitchen.

"How many people are coming to the party?" she asks excitedly.

"I don't know exactly, probably close to eighty."

"How are we going to feed eighty people?"

"What do you mean? We have plenty of food," I say.

"No, I don't mean the amount of food. I mean how are we going to physically feed that many people with no slaves to help? You don't expect me to serve them, do you?" She looks anxious.

I stop what I am doing and stare at her in my usual disbelief.

"Nobody has slaves anymore, Martha Jane. We will put the food out and the guests will help themselves," I explain.

"And," she continues, "What are they going to eat on, pray tell? We don't have good dishes or silver. It's just so...so...embarrassing."

"Embarrassing? I didn't realize my dishes were so beneath you," I say sternly.

"Oh, that's not what I meant. It's just that I

want the party to go well."

I push a basket of corn toward her. "If that's what you want, then roll up your sleeves and help me shuck this corn."

She looks at the basket and then looks up at me like I just slapped her across the face. I almost laugh at the silly expression on her face.

"Well?"

"Um, well, I, eh...I need to go figure out what to do about a new dress and a new bonnet for the party."

"New bonnet?" I ask, stunned.

"Well, don't you think there will be some eligible young men there? I need a new bonnet so I can look my best."

"Martha Jane, you realize we are at war, right?"

She nods.

"You realize all of the eligible young men are off fighting and will not be coming home for this wedding, right?" I continue.

She nods and pouts. She looks down at the table. She looks like I just hurt her feelings and I feel a little sorry for her. I try to make her see reason.

"Martha Jane, no one else will have a new dress or a new bonnet. You will have to re-trim one of your old bonnets and one of your old dresses and make it work."

This information is enough to send her into a full-blown panic. She whines and throws her hands in the air. "How can I attend such a gala in an old dress?"

"Martha Jane, there is no material in the

entire county to make you a new dress!"

She stomps her foot. "Sure, the reason I can't have a new dress is that all of the material was used to bury dead people."

My mouth falls open like a fish gasping for air as I stare at her and try to comprehend what she just said.

She continues, "And what little material there is left is apparently being used to make a wedding dress for Virginia!"

She says the name "Virginia" like it is poison on her lips.

"What? Virginia is the bride!" I am astonished.

"Yes! Exactly. Virginia already has a man. Don't you see? I'm the one who needs a new dress for the party!"

I can't believe Martha Jane is jealous of Virginia's dress, for goodness's sake. I sigh at Martha Jane, shake my head, and go back to my chore.

It is a good thing she stomps out of the room before I do.

Sometimes, that girl is just exhausting.

In two days' time, Virginia and James marry at the church, and William and I host a barn dance at our home following the ceremony. There is music, good food, and lots of family and friends. So many of our friends and neighbors attend, it seems like the old days before the war and the fever. It also feels like this entire community is overdue for a good, old-fashioned barn dance.

As I watch the children interacting, I pull William aside and tell him to get ready to host more dances.

"What do you mean?"

"Well, your daughter, Mary Eliza, has been making eyes at young Richard Blanks all evening."

I nod toward the two talking in the corner. William looks in their direction and eyes the couple with no expression at all.

"And," I continue, "my Mattie has been inseparable from Richard's brother, William Blanks, for the last two hours."

I realize I sound as excited as a school girl gossiping with a girlfriend at my first social. I feel elated at the promise of young love in our midst, and realize for the first time in years that I feel truly hopeful for the future.

William acts like he isn't much impressed with my news, but later in the evening, I see him watching the young couples, and I figure he is sizing up the Blanks brothers to see if they are good enough for his daughter and stepdaughter. I am tickled watching him be the overprotective father.

At one point during the evening, William pulls me out on the dance floor for a slow dance. I'm a little nervous as I haven't danced with anyone since Rice, and that was at our wedding so many years ago. But William is a good dancer and leads me around the floor with ease. He is a kind and loving man, but I can't help but compare him to Rice all the time. I miss Rice so much. It's hard to move on with my life when my life was Rice for sixteen years of marriage and twelve years of childhood before that.

As I think of Rice and the life together we are missing, I notice William wistfully looking down at me. He is so very attentive and notices my melancholy mood immediately.

"Let's go outside and talk," he says, abruptly taking my hand and pulling me to the barn door.

He leads me behind the barn, then sits on the bottom of the split-rail fence and pulls me to him. I stand between his legs and look down at him as he holds my hands in his. In the moonlight, he is a very handsome man, but our relationship is built out of necessity, not romance. Still, I am always very happy in his presence.

"Can we talk about something serious?" he asks.

"Sure, William, of course we can. What's on your mind?"

William looks down and takes a moment to gather his thoughts. "It's just that we have been married a while now, and if you agree, I would like our marriage to be more than a convenience or a necessity. I would like us to really become man and wife."

He looks down at my hands in his as he speaks, and rubs his thumbs across my knuckles. When he finishes, he looks up at me with anticipation written all over his face.

I am a little surprised by his suggestion, and I was hoping that maybe in time this would happen on its own without us pushing it. I really do like him. He is a very, very good man. He is a good provider and a good father and a good husband. He's been by my side through Monroe dying and my mother dying. He was even ready to get into a gunfight with those Yankees over me and my safety. He's almost my Prince Charming, my knight in shining armor.

But, sadly, he is not Rice. He doesn't have Rice's smile. He doesn't have Rice's sandy blonde hair. And most of all, he doesn't give me butterflies the way Rice did. Though I've never really allowed him to try.

As I look down at him, knowing that as a good wife I should agree to become his wife in all ways, he pulls me to him and tenderly kisses me on the lips. I'm a little surprised. He reaches up to the back of my hair and pulls me even harder to him as his kiss becomes more passionate. I close my eyes and allow it to consume me. All I can think is, "Oh, my goodness. Butterflies!"

For a few short hours on this moonlit evening, during the middle of the war and the beginning of an unexpected romance with my husband, life seems happy.

Everyone seems to be enjoying themselves, even though I know in my heart that some are only putting on a front for the benefit of everyone else. For some folks in attendance who have lost so much over the last few years, it is a melancholy kind of evening. They are having a good time, but they are missing their loved ones. Nevertheless, people are smiling, and I can't remember the last time I witnessed that.

At the end of the evening, William and I lie in bed talking about the success of the party, and note that everyone seemed to have a wonderful time, except for one person—my sister, Martha Jane. She did nothing but complain all evening.

Wilson, Hilliard, and John

On a dreary, rainy spring morning, Reverend Jones rides up on his horse and knocks on the door.

"I went into town to get my mail and found this for you. I thought I would bring it to you and save you the trip to town," he says as he pulls a letter from his jacket and hands it to me.

I smile at him and say, "Thank you so much, Reverend. That was so kind of you."

I offer him something to drink, but he declines. He mounts his horse, tips his hat, and rides off through the red mud puddles on the road, saying, "Give Mr. Jolly my regards."

I close the door and sit down at the table, turning the letter over and over. It has no return address, and I have no idea who it is from. I open the mystery letter. It is from my little brother, Wilson.

My dear sister,

I am writing to you from a hospital bed. I would tell you exactly which hospital, but I'm not quite sure where I am. It's more like a tent than a real hospital. I was not injured during fighting, but instead came down with a bad cold. It has turned into some sort of sickness, but the doctors here have been keeping me real comfortable.

I wrote to my wife, Sarah Jane, but since I don't know exactly where I am, I could not ask her to write me back. If I don't make it through this illness, will you please see after her and my daughter? I have not yet seen my little girl, and she's already two years old. If it be God's will, I hope to see her soon.

Thank you for your prayers.

Love,
Your brother,
Wilson Rodgers

I hold the letter to my chest and close my eyes. I say a prayer for Wilson's healing. I then pick up the envelope and turn it over and over but cannot tell where it was mailed from. I wish I could write him back, but it is not to be.

Bad news just keeps coming.

In June, we get word that Rice's brother, Hilliard, was injured in a battle at Dallas, Georgia, and is in the hospital there. Thankfully, he arrives home shortly after the news is received, but in a sad turn of events, he dies in his bed a few weeks later in the arms of his wife.

"Mr. and Mrs. Carpenter must be beside themselves at the loss of yet another child," I tell William.

"Yes, we need to go over and visit them soon."

"I know they would love to see the children. Let's plan to make a day of it in a few weeks," I say.

If that isn't enough sadness to last a lifetime,

in September, I receive a letter postmarked from Jonesboro, Georgia.

Dear Mrs. Mary Jolly,

It is with deep sorrow and regret that I write to inform you of the death of Private John Rodgers. Private Rodgers was shot in the stomach in battle at Jonesboro, Georgia. His company had to move on and left him in our care.

Sadly, we did all that we could for him but could not save him. He had simply lost too much blood on the battlefield before they could get him to us.

With our deepest condolences,
Thomas Sheffield
Chief Field Surgeon
Confederate Hospital Number 4
Jonesboro, Georgia

My heart is again broken. I close my eyes and picture John's face when he was a little boy with dark hair and sparkling blue eyes. He always had that mischievous twinkle in his eye, as if he was just about to play a prank or do something silly. John was the baby boy of our family, the funniest one with the best jokes. I was so proud of the man he became, even though I forever viewed him as a little boy. I was hoping that soon he would return home and marry and live near me.

Goodness knows I am running out of family around me. I have five brothers who are dead, two who live far away, Wilson who is in some unknown hospital, and Hays Jr. who is God knows where, fighting in this war. I think back to the days of wishing for a sister and complaining there were too many boys around. Well, I have sisters now, two who live far away and Martha Jane. In a moment of childish nostalgia, I wish I could travel back in time and take it all back. I would give anything to be surrounded by my brothers again. I cry for a week over John.

I begin to expect bad news daily and feel nothing but sadness. I stick to my routine and go through the motions. I keep the house running smoothly. I cook for William and the children. I pray every day that the bad news will end. I pray that I will someday feel better and that life will become happy again. I don't know how any of that is possible, but I am hopeful. More than anything, I am just thankful Momma and Daddy are not alive to witness all of this death and sorrow. Daddy was always such a strong man, but I imagine the deaths of so many of his sons would have broken him.

Everyone we know has lost a brother, a son, or a husband in the war. And every family we know has been touched by the fever. In the haze of sadness that hangs over our community like a dark cloud, we try to continue with our daily lives and maintain some sort of normalcy. We try to keep up each other's morale by having barbecues and picnics.

On a sunny Sunday afternoon following church service, we attend a community barbecue. Martha Jane meets a handsome Confederate soldier who is home on leave. You would think that Martha

Jane had learned her lesson about being left at home as the wife of a man off fighting in the war, but apparently not. By the end of the week, Martha Jane and the boy are married, and within days of their union, he goes back to fight with his company. I have to admit the boy is dashingly handsome, but I don't know what she is thinking. What surprises me the most is that she married the boy while wearing an old dress.

For a few weeks following the marriage, Martha Jane's spirits improve and she is again bouncing around the house with a smile on her face. But as the reality of her actions starts to hit her, she reverts to her old ways. Martha Jane is again under my feet complaining, but now she is complaining as Mrs. James Meeks, who I am no fonder of than Mrs. Martin Warren.

Not six months after Martha Jane's wedding, we receive a letter saying that James Meeks was killed in battle.

This time, I do not see relief on Martha Jane's face. This time, she is genuinely saddened by this turn of events. She is now twice widowed before the age of twenty, and her future as a wife and mother do not look bright. Her heart and spirit are broken, and my heart is broken for her.

I try to engage her in daily activities, but she just sits on the front porch, staring solemnly into the distant field. I don't know if we will ever get our old Martha Jane back—the bubbly, smiling one, or the complaining one.

December 1864

To my dear sister Mary,

I am writing with some good news and some bad news. I received a letter today from my wife about your hardships over the last two years. I hope you will forgive me for not being there in your time of need. I had hoped this war would be over long, long before now. I think we are living in a very bad time, sister.

Last December, I was promoted to sergeant, so I decided to stay and finish this war, and I re-enlisted back in January. Since then, I've had a little mishap of my own, but because of it, I may be coming home soon to help you out.

Back in July, I took a shot to my arm here in Atlanta and the doctor sent me to the hospital. That is the bad news. It has taken a long time, but I'm doing better now, except that my arm doesn't seem to be working at all. The doctors say it needs some time to heal, but I keep trying to tell them that I don't seem to have any feeling in it. I hope the doctor is right and that it will heal. I don't know how to plow, plant, ride, or hunt with one arm. I guess I will learn if I have to.

The good news is I will probably be home very soon. I don't know if it will be for a furlough or a medical discharge, but I will be there very soon either way. If you need anything right now with your children or James's children, send word over to my wife, Loucinda. I'm sure she will help you.

> *Goodbye for now,*
> *Hays Rodgers Jr.*

On Christmas Eve, we gather in the church for our annual service. William and I, Virginia and James, and all of the children sit together in the front two pews. We have really started to become a close family since our move to William's farm. He reaches over and puts his hand on top of mine while we are waiting for the service to begin. He squeezes my hand gently and I look up at him. He looks at me adoringly and then he winks. I smile back at him. It is nice to see him happy.

The Blanks family sits on the other side of the church, except for Richard and William, who sit on our side behind our daughters, Mary Eliza and Mattie. The energy between the young ones is so thick you can almost cut it with a knife. William doesn't look at all pleased, but I think they are cute. I am thrilled by the promise of young love in our midst.

Mr. and Mrs. Carpenter sit in the back. She looks so sad. I wave to her and mouth to her that I will talk to her after the service is over. She nods.

Mr. and Mrs. Calhoun and Mr. and Mrs. Pace come in and sit next to the Carpenters.

Wilson's wife, Sarah Jane, and their little girl sit behind the Blanks family. The girl is growing up so fast. I feel bad that I didn't spend more time with her when she was a baby, and I vow to make an effort to see her more often, especially since we haven't heard anything else from her father, and I fear the worst.

Hays's wife, Loucinda, comes in with her three children and sits next to Sarah Jane.

Bertie and young Tony Washington wave at me as they enter the church and go into the other room. They are no longer slaves but still don't feel comfortable sitting in the main room.

We begin the church service by singing "O Little Town of Bethlehem," and the reverend leads us in a prayer for our absent fighting men and for our country. Even though this service is a little more solemn than our usual Christmas services, it is still very beautiful.

Following the sermon, we give thanks that the fever has passed and has not come back, and that so many were spared the death it left in its wake. Then we light candles for the loved ones we have lost. I light candles for Rice, Monroe Franklin, Daddy, Momma, and my brothers, Timothy, John, and James. I pause and say a prayer that I won't have to light one for Wilson. I pray that my little brother will be healed and come home soon to be with his wife and little girl. The Carpenters and I light the most candles of any of the families. The room is brighter than a wheat field on a sunny day.

By the end of the service, we all feel a little stronger and a little lighter. We have a solid community here, and war and sickness can take away our breath for days on end, but in the long run, it cannot take away our spirit. And it certainly cannot take away the spirit of Christmas.

We hug and say our goodbyes and get ready to leave the church. Suddenly, a painfully thin and ragged man enters. The voices quiet one by one, and everyone stops to stare at the soiled stranger.

The man looks around and allows his bag to fall from his shoulder onto the floor with a thud. He has holes in his pants legs and the elbows of his jacket. There are no buttons left on his jacket to hold it closed, so he has it tied together with a piece of twine wrapped around his waist. The tops of his shoes also have holes in them and I imagine the bottom soles do, too. His beard has grown down to the middle of his chest and his hair is almost as long. It has large streaks of gray mixed in with the original dark brown color. When he opens his mouth to speak, I look at his blue eyes and gasp.

"Loucinda, do you not recognize your husband? Mary, did you not get my letter that I would be home soon?"

"Oh, my dear Lord in heaven," I whisper and put my hand over my mouth.

It is Hays Jr. It is an older, thinner, very bearded Hays Jr., but it is him nonetheless. In an uncharacteristic move, Loucinda runs over to him and wraps her arms around his neck. We hug him and cry tears of joy. This is the best Christmas present any of us could receive.

The War Is Over

Word spreads like wildfire through the town and the countryside. Church bells ring. News boys shout the news on street corners. The newspaper headline bears four bold words, "The War Is Over!"

I have very mixed feelings about this news. Yes, the war has ended and I am happy about that. But, this also means that the Confederate States of America is finished. Where does that leave us?

We travel down to Meridian to join the celebration. The streets still look awful. Sherman's army devastated this town. Buildings and homes are nothing but rubble. The railroad tracks have been repaired, and a few of the buildings that were not totally burned down have been rebuilt, but it is not the town I remember. There is so much rubble on the streets, one has to be careful where to step.

Regardless of how the town looks, the air is electric with excitement. Most of the women we see in town are saying, "Praise God" under their breath. Most of the men are relieved that it is over but some are infuriated that General Lee surrendered. They are probably frightened by the anticipated lack of freedom and our quickly diminished state's rights. We are certainly facing an uncertain future. We have no town left. We have no crops. We have no slaves. But we all agree that we are glad the war is over.

There is a great feeling of celebration all across the town. People are putting up banners in preparation of welcoming the men home. A boy is selling little American flags on the corner, and people are buying them and waving them incessantly. The few stores that weren't burned to the ground are filled with people exchanging stories and hugs and pats on the back. There is a barbecue and a parade and a band playing happy songs in front of the courthouse. It is indeed a great celebration.

I, however, am not pleased or frightened or celebrating. The North has taken almost everything from me, and I have no more to give. There will be no brother or husband returning home to me. They are all dead—Rice, Hilliard, John, Timothy, Martin Warren, James Meeks, and probably my dear Wilson. The only one who came home is Hays Jr., and he came home with a wilted spirit and a useless arm. I hate to be a stick in the mud, but I refuse to wave the little flag that William buys for me.

My only thought while looking around the devastated streets of Meridian is how fast can we rebuild everything the Yankees destroyed? And will it do any good? The railroad tracks are rebuilt, but how many stores no longer have an owner to rebuild them, and how many farms no longer have slaves or sons in the family to run them? There are no crops to ship anywhere and no one to plant or harvest new crops. In my opinion, our future is very bleak, indeed.

Rebuilding in the South begins immediately and intensely. Many stores in Meridian are rebuilt and reopened as the fighting boys return home.

Work begins in earnest on the farms. The South is beginning its recovery. The one thing in all of this that sparks my interest is that I missed my last flow. I haven't told William yet, but I am quite sure I am carrying his child, and I am very excited to hold another baby in my arms.

On a crisp fall evening, after putting all the children to bed, William and I sit on our front porch, enjoying the coolness.

"William?"

"Yes, my dear," he answers as he lights his pipe.

"I want to thank you for what you've done for me and my children," I begin.

He smiles at me. "It is I who should thank you for everything you've done for me and mine."

I look across the road into the twilight of the field, full of contentment that all of the children are happy and healthy and well cared for.

"Can I ask you a question?"

"Of course," he says.

"How would you feel about having another child?"

William pulls his pipe from his lips and squints his eyes at me.

"Well?" I ask after what seems like an endless moment of silence.

"Mary Ann, I can't even describe how happy that would make me. Are you with child?" He smiles.

"Yes, William, I am. I am due in March." I smile back.

William slowly puts his pipe down, rises

from his chair, and walks over to me. He bends over and rests his hands on the arms of my chair. He leans right into my face and looks me in the eyes.

"Mary Ann, a few short years ago, I thought my life was over. I didn't know how to survive. You brought a new spark into my world and made my life worth living again. I always admired you, but I had no idea how deeply I would fall in love with you. Thank you for being here. Thank you for being you. Thank you for loving me and giving me a new lease on life." He kisses me gently on the lips. "And thank you for giving me a child." He takes my hands and pulls me to my feet. He looks deeply into my eyes and says, "I love you."

I enter the protective circle of his arms, lay my head on his chest, and whisper, "I love you, too, William."

He pulls back a little and I look up at him. He kisses me softly.

When our daughter, Alice, is born in March of 1866, I begin to feel a little hope for the future.

Going Away

Hays Jr. calls a family meeting. We gather around the big table in my kitchen with William and me, Hays and Loucinda, and all of the children. Hays says he would like to make an announcement. He always handles himself like a politician, straightening his jacket and clearing his throat before delivering his big speech. I smile at his air of grandeur.

"I called this family meeting to make an announcement about our future." He motions to his wife and James's children. "And the future of Allen John, Lizzie, Ellen, Willie, and Necie."

I don't know what any of this has to do with James's children, and suddenly feel a sense of anxiety.

He continues, "I don't feel that our economy is going to turn around here very quickly, so Loucinda and I are going to move to Pickens County and join her family in their hog-raising operation. It has become very successful and I think it is the best economic option for us to join them. We will also be closer to our sister, Elizabeth, and her husband, George."

"Hogs? This is about hogs?" I think, my forehead wrinkling with confusion.

He takes a breath and continues. "Since I am

the legal guardian of James's children, I would like to take them to Alabama with me."

What?! I feel as if someone just sucked all the air out of the room. Alabama? Sometimes I hate being a woman with no say-so, but since Hays is my little brother, I think I can fight him on this decision. I gather my thoughts, take a breath, and start to say that I disagree with his decision, but William reaches under the table and puts his hand on my leg to stop me from turning this into a fight in front of the children. I glance over at him and he gives me the slightest shake of his head. I quickly realize William is right, and I bite my tongue.

"Alabama?" I ask weakly. "Please continue."

Hays pauses when he looks at me, knowing by the expression on my face that I am not happy with him or his decision.

He finally says, "I know you have been the one raising James's children for the last four years, but if you think about it, they could probably use a fresh start in a new place. In my opinion, for their health and happiness, they need to live in a place that doesn't have this air of sorrow and despair hanging over it like a big thunderhead."

I ponder if Hays Jr. might be right, though it would break my heart in two to lose the children. And I'm not sure that uprooting them and taking them to Alabama is in their best interest.

Before I can speak up, James's eldest son, Allen John, stands up straight and tall with the tips of his fingers on the table. He clears his throat and looks at me.

"Aunt Mary, I don't mean any disrespect to

Uncle Hays, but I have been talking with Uncle Elisha and Uncle Ben about going on a wagon train with them to Texas. I haven't really had the courage to ask you until now, but I am seventeen, almost eighteen, and I think I should be allowed, as a man, to make my own decision about where I would like to live."

He looks at Hays. "I don't mean any disrespect, Uncle Hays, Aunt Loucinda, but I do not want to move to Alabama."

He freezes and awaits a response. Hays and I look at each other. He raises his eyebrows to me, as if asking if I know about this Texas move. I shrug to indicate I don't know a thing about it.

Allen John's little brother, Willie, sits next to him and nods at his brother's every word.

"Do you want to go to Texas, too, Willie?" I ask him, expecting him to look away.

Willie has always been quiet and shy and relied on his older brother to lead him.

"Yes, ma'am." He beams at me.

He does not look down at the floor nor does he look away. He keeps direct eye contact with me. This twelve-year-old is becoming quite a man right in front of my eyes, and that thought brings a little smile to my face. I wink at him.

Allen John sits back down with a look of anticipation.

"Well, now that we're bringing this all up," interrupts Lizzie, her hands clasped in front of her on the table. "I didn't want to say anything without David being here, but we would like to get married." Lizzie has been seeing David Morrow for a while, and I expected this revelation. I am not surprised by what she says next.

"I am almost sixteen and David is twenty-four and making a good living. He has asked me if I would like to be his wife and he plans on asking you, Aunt Mary, very soon. I don't want to go to Alabama, either."

I don't say anything. I just look at them one by one. When my gaze falls on Ellen, I ask her, "And what do you think, Ellen?"

She contemplates for a moment and then says, "I think I would like to go with Uncle Hays and Aunt Loucinda for a while. I would love to see Aunt Elizabeth and Uncle George and their babies. I would not like to go forever, maybe just for a little while. I mean, if it's okay with you, Aunt Mary."

She stumbles over her last words, probably hoping to avoid hurting anyone's feelings, but her face is bright with anticipation of an exciting adventure in a new place.

I sit there in stunned silence, looking from one to the other of them and back again.

"Alabama? Texas? Marriage? So, everyone is going to leave me at the same time? What about you, Necie? Where do you want to go?" I am half teasing and half frightened that she will want to leave, too.

"Nowhere, Aunt Mary. I don't want to go nowhere. I want to stay here with you," she says, as she hurries around the table and wraps her arms around my waist.

"Won't you be sad if your brothers and sisters live somewhere else without you?" I ask, trying to use her as a little leverage to keep the other children from leaving.

She looks from her two sisters to her two brothers, then a little nervously at Hays and Loucinda. Then she turns and looks me right in the eye.

"I will miss them, but I want to stay here." She smiles and kisses me on the cheek.

I pat Necie on the back, take a deep breath and exhale. Necie crawls up into my lap as if I am her protector and as long as she is in my arms, she won't have to go to Alabama.

I look at Hays. "What do you know about this Texas talk?"

"This is the first I've heard of it and I am just as stunned as you are, but if you want me to, I will go to Elisha and Ben tomorrow and get all the details."

We decide to adjourn our meeting until tomorrow night and will decide at that time what is best for the children.

Allen John reminds us once again that he is almost eighteen and should be able to make the decision for himself.

Hays reminds him that he is still only seventeen and under Hays's guardianship.

* * *

Within a few short months, we have a huge going away party for Allen John and Willie. The next morning, we hook up the oxen to the wagon and send the boys off with their uncles in style, albeit with tears and fears. I make them promise to write to me often and tell me of their adventures. I hug and kiss them both on their cheeks. Willie hugs me back long and hard, but Allen John is already climbing into the driver's seat, ready to go. He is a hardheaded boy with an attitude as big as Texas, but when I see him lean over and help his little brother up onto the wagon, I see a glimpse of his overprotective father in him and I smile. I know in my heart they will be just fine.

As a sad tear rolls down my cheek, I glance up to the sky and silently tell James that he should be proud of his boys. I beg him to watch over them.

The next morning, Hays and Loucinda load their children and James's daughter, Ellen, into their wagon for the move to Alabama. Ellen promises that she is just going for a little while, not forever, and she will be back soon. I try not to cry as I tell her to give her aunt Elizabeth a big hug for me.

Lizzie is given our blessing to marry David Morrow, but not until next year when she turns seventeen. She is not too happy with that plan, but there is not much she can do about it.

When little Necie absolutely refuses to go with Hays, we decide that since I am the only mother Necie can remember, it is probably best she stay with me. Thank the good Lord that my brother listened to reason. It would break my heart to lose Necie.

The only family I have left in Mississippi besides Martha Jane is my brother, Allen, and he is all the way up in Carroll County. Lewis is in Texas, and soon my nephews will be there, too. Susannah is in Louisiana. Elizabeth and now Hays are in

Alabama. Martha Jane and I are the last of Daddy's children in Lauderdale County. The only thing that keeps depression from setting in is the fact it is going to be a busy year for I am again with child.

William's daughter, Mary Eliza, agrees to marry Richard Blanks. I don't think William is overjoyed about either of the Blanks boys, but his daughter is happy and in love so he gives her his blessing. Now I have a pregnancy and Mary Eliza's weddings to plan. William speaks with Lizzie's boyfriend and puts off their wedding until next year when Lizzie is older. But there isn't much he can do to postpone Mary Eliza's wedding. She and Richard are old enough to marry without William's permission, so we start planning their wedding immediately.

In January, we celebrate their marriage with a church ceremony and a barbecue at our house. Richard hires a real band to play at the party and everyone dances late into the night. Every person I know is in attendance, and everyone says it is the best party they have ever been to.

Spring is a good time to have a baby and it is just around the corner. In May, my pretty Sarah Louella is born. She is perfect, with a head full of dark hair and pretty little hands.

Between throwing weddings, helping little Alice learn to walk, and taking care of baby Sarah Louella, I don't even notice how much time my eldest daughter, Mattie, is spending with young William Blanks. I am blindsided when he comes to my husband and me to ask for Mattie's hand in marriage.

I am not sure how I feel about Mattie marrying. I like William Blanks, and I never had a problem marrying off any of the other children, but Mattie is my firstborn. I birth children. I raise children. I bury children. I even let children move to other parts of the country. But I have never before given permission for my firstborn to marry and leave the family home.

Time flies. It seems like only yesterday Mattie was a baby, and now she is eighteen. Has it really been that long since Rice gazed so lovingly at his baby girl with such pride and excitement for the future? So many things have happened in the last eighteen years. So many things have changed. The only thing I can figure as I try to understand my feelings is this means I am getting older, too. I will now become the grandmother when Mattie becomes the mother, and everyone will take a step forward. No matter what happens, time keeps moving forward.

As I come to grips with Mattie's marriage, I feel quite happy for her and young William Blanks. I say a prayer for them, wishing them a long and happy life together.

They are married on November 1st, and my wonderful husband spares no expense in throwing them the biggest and best of parties.

Beginnings and Endings

In the spring of 1869, at the age of forty, I am again with child. I love children and consider myself extremely blessed by the good Lord to be carrying another child, but at my age, I sincerely hope that this will be my last. Running after two-year-old Sarah Louella and three-year-old Alice requires a little more energy than I have to give nowadays. This baby will be my eighth child by birth and the seventeenth I've raised by the blessings of God, so I know how busy I will be the next few months and years. I make a decision to really focus on enjoying and treasuring each and every moment, because it will hopefully be the last time I will experience any of it.

I'm sitting on the front porch in my rocking chair, thinking about my coming child, when Mattie unexpectedly pulls up to the house in her wagon and comes up to sit by me.

After we make small talk for an hour, she blurts out, "Momma, I actually came over to tell you something important." She fidgets with her bonnet on her lap.

"What is it?" I wonder what in the world she is so nervous about.

She takes a deep breath and announces, "I am with child."

I jump up and hug her. "What great news! Congratulations!"

I sit back down and start to laugh. She looks at me like I have lost my mind.

"What is so funny?" she asks.

"Oh, it's not you I'm laughing at, honey."

"Good, because this isn't funny. I'm a little scared."

"Scared about what?"

"The whole thing. Birthing a baby and then being responsible for another human being for the rest of my life."

"Mattie, you'll be fine. It's a very natural thing. You've taken care of babies before and when it's your own, it's even better. You'll see. It will be easy for you, and of course I am here to help if you need me."

She relaxes a little bit and looks out across the yard and the road into the field. She is suddenly lost in thought and I let her think for a while.

After a few minutes, I say, "Me, too."

"Me, too, what?"

"I am with child also."

She looks surprised and starts laughing.

We share a wonderful afternoon talking about birthing and child rearing. She asks a million questions about babies and being a mother. She has taken care of many newborns, but is insecure about raising her own child. We bond in a way we haven't in a long time. By the time she leaves, all of her nervousness is gone and she is looking forward to the amazing experience.

As spring gives way to the heat of summer,

Hays Jr. comes back into town to settle our daddy's estate. Daddy's house has been sitting empty for six years since Momma died in '63. We wanted to wait until all of the boys were back from the war before settling it, but it has been seven years since we heard from Timothy and four years since we heard from Wilson, so it is painfully obvious they are not coming back.

Daddy's six hundred and eighty acres of land, along with his home and farm equipment, are worth considerable money. He also held shares of stock in the Mobile and Ohio Railroad, but there is no way to divide all of that up between Lewis in Texas, Susannah in Louisiana, Elizabeth and Hays in Alabama, James's five orphans scattered in three states, Wilson's widow and daughter, Allen, Martha Jane, and me. We decide to ask the court to appoint appraisers and have the property sold so we can split the proceeds.

When court proceedings are over, we sell Daddy's home and all of the land to Major Adam T. Stennis on the steps of the Meridian courthouse. The sale includes the carriage house, the barn and stable, and the smokehouse.

When the coolness of fall arrives, Mattie and I deliver our babies a week apart. She has a girl and names her Ida Francis Blanks. I have a boy and name him John Eades Jolly, John after my dear brother, and Eades is William's middle name. Both babies have the Rodgers' dark hair and blue eyes.

Ida, being my first grandchild, is so precious to me. John, being my first son with William, is just as special. My heart is overflowing with love and happiness. I feel blessed and fulfilled.

Mattie comes over daily to let the babies play together. She occasionally watches them, along with toddlers Alice and Sarah Louella, while I work in the garden or do the wash. Sometimes I watch the children while she goes into town to do some shopping.

Ida and John play together almost every day from the day they are born. They are like twins in how inseparable they are.

Okatibbee Creek

When the sale of Daddy's property is finalized, I take a ride out to the house by myself to look around and sit on that beautiful porch one last time. As soon as I sit down on the front steps, I start crying. Daddy put so much love and pride into this home, and for what? Did it really do any good? Did it really mean anything to anyone?

I sit for a long time and think about Daddy's life, my life, and the meaning of life in general. My first vivid memory is of the day my brothers William and Stephen died, which is the same day my brother, Wilson, was born. I've grown up with some confusion about life and death because of that experience. I was too young at the time to comprehend what happened that day, and I still don't really understand how God can bring one life into the world on the same day he takes two lives out of it. There has to be some kind of plan, right? Or is it just random? So many people from my life are gone now. Why do some people live such a short time? I wish I could find some rational answers, but I don't think there are any.

I think back to William and Stephen's funeral and all the things the reverend said that day. "A life isn't worth anything if there is no one to notice it."

"Well, I've noticed, Daddy," I say through my

tears. "I noticed your life, your work ethic, and the love you gave to your family. It is now being passed down through generations. Your children share your morals and values. Your grandchildren are growing up with the love that you planted as tiny seeds in all of us. More than likely, your great grandchildren, who won't even know you, will still grow up with high standards and values because of you and your love."

I look up and see Bertie slowly walking up the road toward the house. She's wearing a dark blue dress and a floppy straw hat covering her eyes.

"Hi, Miss Bertie," I yell to her as I wipe away my tears and put a smile on my face.

"Hi, baby girl." She waves back.

"What brings you out on this lovely morning?" I ask when she finally reaches the porch and plops down on the step. She takes off her hat and reveals her gray hair tied in a bun. She sets her hat next to her and wipes beads of sweat off her forehead with her handkerchief.

"I was just on my way to your house to see the babies and to see how you are doing," she says as she tucks her handkerchief back into her sleeve.

I can tell by her demeanor that there is something more on her mind, but I figure she will tell me when she is ready.

"Well, it's nice to see you. We are all doing fine at home," I reply.

"That's good to hear, baby girl."

"Bertie, I'm forty-one years old. How long are you going to call me baby girl?" I tease her.

She laughs. "You have been my baby girl

since I came to your daddy's house when you were six years old. You will always be my baby girl."

"Aw, you know I love you, Miss Bertie." I reach over and pat her bony hand.

"And I love you, too, baby girl. You know, you have always been the smartest and most beautiful of your momma's children. And with everything you have been through, you have become the strongest and most courageous woman I have ever known."

She pauses and looks out across the yard as her mind wanders to another time and place.

After a moment she adds, "Your momma and daddy would be very proud of you, but it was a blessing they were not around to witness all the pain and loss we went through."

She pauses again and looks out across the yard. "You're also a wonderful mother."

I can tell she's leading up to something.

"I don't know what I would have done without you, Bertie. You helped me through so much."

"I know what you went through, baby girl. I witnessed it all. I have seen you stand strong in the face of disaster and death and sickness and hunger. You have faced every adversity with courage and every defeat with dignity and grace. I'm very proud of you, more than you'll ever know."

My eyes well up with tears as I feel a mixture of being touched by her kind words, and trepidation that she is going somewhere awful with this talk.

"Bertie, your love has been one of the reasons I have been able to be strong and steadfast. Together, we have laughed and cried through so much," I say as I stare straight ahead at the field.

Memories come flooding back, along with the sadness and the happiness. Rice, Daddy, Momma, Monroe Franklin. I shake the memories off and look back at Bertie.

"I have the feeling you weren't headed all the way to my house just to tell me you're proud of me." I stop and wait for her to speak.

"Well, baby girl, like I said, you have always been the smartest of your momma's children." She takes a deep breath and exhales. I wait patiently as I watch her build up her courage.

"Well, I have not been feeling very well lately and I saw the doctor. He said he can't do much for me and I may not be around much longer. You know I have raised Tony as my own since his parents died of the fever. He's only thirteen and not quite ready to face the world on his own just yet."

She looks away. I can tell she is trying to get through this speech without crying. Finally, she turns to me and looks me straight in the eye.

"I want to ask you to take care of Tony when my time comes. I can rest easy if I know you will do that for me."

"What? Bertie, of course I will take care of Tony. But I don't want to hear anything about you being gone. We've been through too much together and everything finally seems to be turning around for the better."

I pause, wondering if that is really true. Is everything going to be all right?

I continue, "We've walked straight through

the midst of hell and we are just now starting to find our way back."

"I hope you're right, baby girl, but we can't control what the good Lord wants to do. We just have to handle it the best we can when it comes."

I nod and quietly say, "Bertie, I will do whatever you need me to do."

"I know you will, baby girl. I just thought it would be nice to ask." She winks at me.

Using both arms to lift herself, Bertie slowly rises from the step. I stand up, too, and she gives me a long hug. She puts her hat on and carefully steps away from the porch, heading toward the dirt road. I yell "goodbye" to her and she waves her hand behind her head without turning around. She walks very, very slowly, favoring one leg more than the other, and I watch her until she shuffles out of sight. I replay the conversation over and over again in my mind.

When I finally decide to leave, I turn around and look at the house one last time. I picture it when it was a bustling farm and Daddy was a happy man. I can see him working out in the field. I can see the smoke coming from the chimney and smell the pork from the smokehouse. I can see Bertie and Momma sitting on the front porch working on their embroidery. It was a happy home, if only for a few short years.

As I mount my horse to leave, William rides up. "What are you doing out here?" I smile at the nice surprise.

"Martha Jane told me you took a ride out here to reminisce and I thought you might need a shoulder."

"That is so sweet of you. I'm all right. I just really wanted to come out here and say goodbye. This land holds so many memories, and I just can't sell it off without taking a minute to...I don't know, what is the word?" I pause for a moment. "Witness. That's the word. I wanted to come here and be a witness for my dear daddy, who put his blood and sweat into this land and turned it into something wonderful."

William looks at me tenderly.

"You are an amazing woman, Mary."

I smile at him through my tears.

"And you are an amazing man, William. You always know the right time to show up and be supportive."

"Right place at the right time," he grins. "Are you ready to go?"

I nod.

"Do you want to ride down by the creek on our way home?" he asks.

"Yes, I would like that very much."

When we arrive at Okatibbee Creek, the afternoon sun is finding its way through the treetops and glistening on the water like floating diamonds. We dismount and have a seat not far from the clearing where my brothers died so many years ago. It is also the same place Rice first kissed me and asked me to marry him. This creek holds so many memories, good and bad, but mostly good.

We sit quietly next to each other on the bank, listening to the sounds of the birds and the rippling water washing up on the rocks. I think that this creek is a lot like the seeds of love Daddy planted in us. It may change form over time, but it is always here. Daddy's love and this creek may be the only constant things I have. People come and go, babies are born, lives are lost, but this creek is always here. I wonder how many generations have enjoyed this place. I wonder how many more generations will sit in this clearing and swim in this water. How many more first kisses will be shared on these banks?

My thoughts turn again to the words from the sermon at my brothers' funeral so many years ago. That sermon has haunted me my whole life, and I think I finally understand it.

Our only duty in this life is to be available as a witness to each other's lives. When my daddy died, so did my entire childhood. When Rice died, so did my first love and the experiences of having my first children. We need to share our time and love with those around us right now, not knowing if our time together will be long or very, very short. By doing this, we say through unspoken words, "I will be your witness. You will not have lived in vain for I was there and I noticed."

I sit and watch the rippling water for a long time. I hope that my children and grandchildren will grow up to be witnesses for each other. And I promise myself that one day I will tell them all we have been through, in the hopes they will never take one moment of life, love, or family for granted. I hope they will pass on our story to their children so that someday all of our descendants will know we were here.

Finally breaking the silence, I say softly,

"William."

He looks at me without answering.

"I love you."

The End

Author's Notes

Okatibbee Creek (pronounced oh-kuh-TIB-be) is a story of historical fiction. It is the story of my third great-grandparents, Mary Ann Rodgers and Rice Benjamin Carpenter, as I imagine the way their lives unfolded. It has been emotionally challenging and rewarding bringing their story to life. The dates, places, and names are historically accurate, but the personalities and details of their experiences are fictitious.

There are a few minor historical liberties I have taken:

The Sunday church service in 1834 in the second chapter is fictitious. Fellowship Baptist Church was not established until 1836, and the church met for a time in member's homes before meeting in the gum-log cabin.

The drowning deaths of Mary Ann's brothers, William and Stephen, are fictitious. They both died in 1834 at the ages of eight and ten, but the circumstances surrounding their deaths are unknown.

The name of Mary Ann and Rice's youngest son is not known. The Jolly family bible states his initials were M.F. I chose the name Monroe Franklin after Mary Ann's nephews: James Monroe Chatham, son of Susannah; and William Franklin Rodgers, son of Allen.

There is no historical evidence of a typhoid epidemic in Lauderdale County during the winter of 1862-63. The only facts are that typhoid was rampant at that time, and there are too many deaths in the family timed too closely together to justify coincidence.

The slave stories included in this book are referenced from "*The First Hundred Years of the Pine Springs Community*" by Mary Ellen New White. The original accounts did not involve the Rodgers or Carpenter families. And Bertie and Old Sam are products of my imagination.

An enormous thank you to family, friends, and associates who helped with research, pictures, time, encouragement, and patience as this book was written. In alphabetical order by first name:

Cate Caldwell - *independent film writer /producer/ director*

Dana Butler - *descendant of Susannah Rodgers Chatham*

David Hill - *Past Commander, Louisiana Division, Sons of Confederate Veterans*

Debra Bradley Wines - *fellow writer*

Elyse Dinh-McCrillis - *TheEditNinja.com*

Gail Fuller - *descendant of Mary Ann Rodgers*

Jennifer Maginn Bauer - *descendant of James Rodgers*

Jen Quist - *JenQPhotography.com*

Jonathan Hess - *fellow writer*

Martha Wise - *descendant of James Rodgers*

Maxey Baucum - *family genealogist and Civil War buff*

Robert Bryant Jarman, Sr. - *friend of Jolly descendants*

Robert Hess – *book designer*

Sharron B. McAvoy - *descendant of Mary Ann Rodgers*

Photos

Mary Ann's father: Hays Rodgers, Sr.
February 1, 1793-December 1862
Son of James Rodgers and Elizabeth "Elly"
Hays

Mary Ann's brother:
Hays Rodgers Jr. and wife Loucinda Graham
November 1, 1832-June 22, 1913

Mary Ann's sister:
Elizabeth Rodgers and husband George
Graham (brother of Loucinda Graham Rodgers)
January 26, 1839-September 19, 1875

The "Ole Stennis House" in Lauderdale County, MS, built by Hays Rodgers, Sr. in 1857. Following his death in 1862 and probate court in 1869, the home was sold at auction to Major Adam T. Stennis on the steps of the Meridian courthouse. It remained in the Stennis family for over one hundred years and is currently owned by the Hover family.

(Author photo, April 2012)

Mary Ann's eldest child:
Martha Lettie "Mattie" Carpenter Blanks
December 10, 1848-January 31, 1933
(Photo courtesy of Gail Fuller, descendant of
Mary Ann Rodgers)

Martha Lettie "Mattie" Carpenter Blanks and
husband William Henry Blanks III
(Photo courtesy of Gail Fuller, descendant of
Mary Ann Rodgers)

Mary Ann's youngest son:
John Eades Jolly and wife Sarah Elizabeth
Johnson on their wedding day 1894
December 17, 1869-1943
(Photo courtesy of Robert Bryant Jarman, Sr.)

Mary Ann's daughter:
Alice Jolly Williamson (on far right) and
family
March 27, 1866-December 28, 1919
(Photo courtesy of Sharron B. McAvoy,
descendant of Mary Ann Rodgers)

Mary Ann's daughter:
Sarah Louella "Ludie" Jolly Williamson and
family
May 12, 1867-September 20, 1952
(Photo courtesy of Sharron B. McAvoy,
descendant of Mary Ann Rodgers)

Mary Ann's nephew (James's son):
Allen John Rodgers (seated with beard) and
wife Margaret Turner
with their children and grandchildren in
Texas about 1906
March 1849-April 15, 1914
(Photo courtesy of Jennifer Maginn Bauer,
descendant of James Rodgers)

Mary Ann's niece (James's daughter): Martha
Ellen Rodgers Meek
April 4, 1853-August 13, 1890
(Photo courtesy of Martha Wise, descendant
of James Rodgers)

Mary Ann's first husband:
Rice Benjamin Carpenter, Confederate military record
August 15, 1828-December 31, 1862

Mary Ann's brother:
Hays Rodgers Jr., Confederate military record

Mary Ann's brother:
Timothy Rodgers, Confederate military record
April 4, 1830-Last heard from 1862

Mary Ann's brother:
John W. Rodgers, Confederate military record
November 9, 1836-September 1, 1864

Mary Ann's brother:
Wilson Rodgers, Confederate military record
September 2, 1834-Last heard from 1864

Mary Ann's brother-in-law (Rice's brother): Hilliard Carpenter, Confederate military record
January 19, 1817-July 16, 1864

(Confederate.)

C | 2 Cav. | Miss.

H Carpenter

Pvt., Co. C, 2 Reg't Mississippi Cavalry.

Appears on

Company Muster Roll

of the organization named above,

for .... July & Aug 1864

Enlisted:
When .... Aug 29, 1863.
Where Columbus
By whom Capt Rogers
Period 3 yro

Last paid:
By whom Capt Dashiell
To what time .... Oct 31, 1863.

Present or absent ....
Remarks: died at home
July 16, 1864, from
wounds recd May
28 '64

Mary Ann's brother-in-law (Martha Jane's husband):
Martin V. Warren, Confederate military record
1842-February 20, 1863

```
                    ( CONFEDERATE. )

  W              8                    Miss


   M. V. Warren

   Pvt   Co. H. 8th Miss Regt


Appears on a
                     LIST
of killed and wounded, of Jackson's
Brigade, Army of Tenn., during the
actions near Murfreesboro, Tenn.,
between Dec. 30, 1862, and Jan. 3,
1863.
List dated Chattanooga
                      Jan 12    , 1863 .

Remarks: Wounded severely in face
```

Mary Ann's nephew (Susannah's son): James Monroe Chatham, Confederate military record
1842-October 28, 1861

Mary Ann's nephew (Susannah's son): James
Monroe Chatham 1842-October 28, 1861
Camp Moore Confederate Cemetery
Tangipahoa, Louisiana
(Photo courtesy of David Hill, Past
Commander, Louisiana Division, Sons of
Confederate Veterans)

Mary Ann's second husband:
William Eades Jolly
December 14, 1817-March 15, 1890
Memorial Park Cemetery
Union, Newton County, Mississippi
(Photo courtesy of Dianna Albertson)

Mary Ann Rodgers Carpenter Jolly
March 17, 1828-July 18, 1898
Bethel Cemetery
Nellieburg, Lauderdale County, Mississippi
(Author photo, April 2012)

References

1850, 1860, and 1870 US census and 1853 Mississippi census
www.Ancestry.com

Civil War Battle of Stones Creek / Murfreesboro
www.civilwarhome.com/stones.html

Company Rosters of the Civil War Companies Raised in Lauderdale County, Mississippi
www.lauderdalecoms.com

The First Hundred Years of the Pine Springs Community of Lauderdale County, Mississippi
by Mary Ellen New White
www.kithandkinofthesouth.org

Fold3-Historical Military Records
www.fold3.com

Letters to Jane
by Joelyn Kemp James
Lauderdale County Department of Archives and History, Inc.

P.O. Box 5511
Meridian, MS 39302

Plantation Diary: January-July 1859
by H. Blackwood, overseer, BF Moore
Plantation
Lauderdale County Department of Archives
and History, Inc.

Windows to Our Past: Collinsville, Martin, and Schamberville Communities.
Lauderdale County Department of Archives
and History, Inc.

About the Author

Lori Crane was born in Meridian, Mississippi and now lives in greater Nashville, Tennessee. She has been a life-long fan and student of genealogy after growing up without her father, and as the years passed, she became more and more obsessed with knowing everything possible about her roots. She became fascinated with the story of her third great grandmother Mary Ann Rodgers in April 2012 after visiting her grave in Mississippi.

Her lineage to Mary Ann is: mother Linda Faye Culpepper Crane, grandfather Earl Wilmar Culpepper, great grandmother Annie Josephine Blanks Culpepper, second great grandparents Martha Lettie "Mattie" Carpenter Blanks and William Henry Blanks III, third great grandparents Mary Ann Rodgers Carpenter Jolly and Rice Benjamin Carpenter.

Lori is a member of the Daughters of the American Revolution, the United States Daughters of 1812, and the United Daughters of the Confederacy. She is also a professional musician and a member of the Screen Actors Guild-American Federation of Radio and Television Artists.

Okatibbee Creek was honored with the bronze medal in literary fiction at the 2013 eLit Book Awards. It was also named as an honorable mention in historical fiction at the 2013 Midwest Book Festival.

Lori's other literary awards include being named a finalist in the 2014 Eric Hoffer Awards for *An Orphan's Heart*. Her book, *Elly Hays*, achieved honorable mention in general fiction at the 2013 Midwest Book Festival and was named on the shortlist for "50 Self-published Books Worth Reading in 2013/14" at Indie Author Land. *Elly Hays* debuted at #1 on Amazon Kindle in Native American stories.

Please visit Lori's website at
www.LoriCrane.com

Books by Lori Crane

Okatibbee Creek Series

Okatibbee Creek
An Orphan's Heart
Elly Hays

Stuckey's Bridge Trilogy

The Legend of Stuckey's Bridge
Stuckey's Legacy: The Legend Continues
Stuckey's Gold: The Curse of Lake Juzan

Culpepper Saga

I, John Culpepper
John Culpepper the Merchant
John Culpepper, Esquire
Culpepper's Rebellion

Other Titles

Savannah's Bluebird
Witch Dance
The Culpepper-Fairfax Scandal
On This Day: A Perpetual Calendar for
Family Genealogy

For more information, please visit
www.LoriCrane.com
or email
LoriCraneAuthor@gmail.com.

The following is an excerpt from

"An Orphan's Heart"

The second book in the Okatibbee Creek series

Chapter 1

I don't know how long I've been standing here staring at these mounds of dirt. A few minutes? An hour? I have no idea. Time doesn't have any meaning. The funeral is over, and I'm the only one still here.

I look down the row of pine trees lining the dirt road, and see my sister Lizzie walking arm in arm with her friend David. I place my palm over my brow to shield my eyes from the glaring sun. I spot my brothers and baby sister, Necie, standing in the middle of the road, talking to Aunt Mary. I watch Aunt Mary pick up Necie and place her on her hip.

Poor little Necie doesn't even know what's happening. She keeps asking everyone where Momma is, which breaks my heart. How can she understand something like this at the age of four? I don't understand it myself. I guess it's a good thing she doesn't know we just put Momma in the ground next to Daddy.

We buried Daddy last week. Actually, *we* didn't bury him. Aunt Mary found him dead in the bed next to Momma and had my uncles sneak him out of the house while Momma was unconscious with a fever. I shiver at the thought. Aunt Mary kept us all busy in the garden while the men took Daddy away. They drove him down to the cemetery in the back of a wagon and buried him, and we didn't get to say goodbye. A mound of dirt is still piled high on his grave.

There are two mounds now.

I overheard Aunt Mary tell Aunt Martha Jane that the doctor said Momma and Daddy had typhoid fever. I don't know what that is, but it killed both my parents.

I stand alone in a forest of headstones and wonder how long I can stand here before anyone notices — probably all night. Maybe they would miss me if I didn't show up for breakfast. Maybe not.

That's the problem with being the middle child — not many people notice you. They notice the oldest: "Oh, look how big you've grown!" They notice the youngest: "Aren't you the cutest little thing?" But they don't notice you if you're in the middle. It's like being invisible.

Aunt Mary, with Necie cradled on her hip, leans her head to let Necie play with her hair for a moment. She then looks down at my brother Allen John and wraps her free arm around his shoulder, and they all start walking in the direction of Aunt Mary's house. My six-year-old little brother, Willie, walks on the same side as Necie, holding on to Aunt Mary's skirt with his dirty little fingers. I'd better follow them or I'll be left here alone in the graveyard when night falls.

I take one last look at the mounds of dirt

covering the bodies of my parents, and I shed a single tear. I try to picture Daddy's face but it seems fuzzy, like a dream. I try to imagine Momma's warm smile and loving eyes, but I can't bring them into focus.

Suddenly, a black crow flies overhead and startles me with its loud "Caw!" The sound makes me jump. I wipe the tear away with the back of my hand as I turn and follow my siblings toward Aunt Mary's house.